# Death at Westminster

London Cosy Mysteries
Book 1

Rachel McLean

Millie Ravensworth

ACKROYD
PUBLISHING

Copyright © 2023 by Rachel McLean and Millie Ravensworth

All rights reserved.

No part of this book may be reproduced in any form or by any electronic or mechanical means, including information storage and retrieval systems, without written permission from the author, except for the use of brief quotations in a book review.

This is a work of fiction. Names, characters, businesses, places, events and incidents are either the products of the author's imagination or used in a fictitious manner. Any resemblance to actual persons, living or dead, or actual events is purely coincidental.

Ackroyd Publishing

ackroyd-publishing.com

🌸 Created with Vellum

# Death at Westminster

# Chapter One

Diana Bakewell smiled as the teenage students of Foxwood Grange Academy jostled for the best seats on the tour bus. The bus was a vintage open top Routemaster, a classic red double-decker with the open entrance at the rear, which meant that the automatic assumption that the back seat was the best spot was turned on its head. The seventeen- and eighteen-year-olds clattered upstairs, yelling between themselves about where they would sit in their various groups.

"Would you go and settle them in upstairs, Zaf?" Diana said.

"Sure," replied her assistant tour guide.

Diana watched him climb the stairs and wondered if he wasn't a little tired. Zaf Williams normally reminded her of a rubber bouncy ball with his irrepressible and slightly chaotic energy, but not today.

Diana picked up the microphone as the bus pulled away from the tour group's Marylebone hotel.

"Good morning, ladies and gents. I hope you enjoyed your

breakfast. Welcome aboard this Chartwell and Crouch tour bus, which will be your second home for the week. While our driver Newton takes us on the short journey to the Palace of Westminster, Zaf and I will point out some places of interest as we go, and of course you can ask us any questions about the day's plans."

Addressing them like adults was a deliberate strategy. As far as Diana was concerned, they *were* adults, although she had heard the two teachers haranguing the group as if they were primary school kids while herding them out of the hotel.

A hand went up.

"Yes?" Diana fished around in her mind for the brown-haired student's name. "You have a question, Ava?"

"Can we take photos in the Houses of Parliament?"

Diana nodded. "There *are* rules about photographs in the Palace of Westminster—"

"But what about the Houses of Parliament?" snapped another girl, one seat over.

"They're the same thing," replied Diana. "There are some initial areas where you may take photos, but further inside it's not allowed. It is important to remember that it's a place of work."

"Why are you asking boring suck-up questions, Ava?" muttered a young man a row behind her.

"Because I'm not a moron, Ethan. Go on, you try asking a really interesting question. Bring your A-game."

"Fine." Ethan looked at Diana. "How much do you earn, Miss?"

Diana laughed. "You'd be surprised if I told you, but I reckon the question is off-limits." She glanced over at the two teachers, Mrs Swinburne and Mr Chaplin, but they had their heads down, absorbed in their phone screens.

After thirty years in the tour guide business, Diana had seen all sorts, and she could tell Swinburne and Chaplin were happy to hand over all responsibility for the tour to Diana. Even if they were supposedly in charge.

Zaf clattered down the stairs and gave Diana a thumbs-up from the rear of the bus.

"We have young, enquiring minds, Miss," said Ethan. "No question is off-limits." He jerked a thumb towards Zaf. "So is he your son or your boyfriend?"

Diana gave him a look. Diana, despite some interesting European ancestry, was white and very much a Londoner. Zaf Williams, more than forty years her junior, was black with a Birmingham accent.

"Pleased though that would make me, Zaf isn't my son," replied Diana.

"And she's not my boyfriend," added Zaf.

"Lord, no. I don't think I could compete with that handsome young — Malachi, was it?" Diana said.

But Zaf was shaking his head. *That's why his mood is so subdued*, Diana thought. But tours didn't stop for personal upsets. The show must go on, and all that.

The eager young woman had her hand up again. "Are we meeting the MP today?"

Diana nodded. "Your trip this week is sponsored by your Member of Parliament. It's an initiative called *Our Parliament*, intended to open up the workings of democracy to young people. Your week will consist of—"

"Wait, are you saying that political stuff is all we're seeing on this trip?" asked Ethan. "No shopping or London Eye?"

Diana glanced again at the teachers, wondering if they'd told the students anything about the visit in advance. They continued to stare downwards, as if nothing was happening.

"I'm sure you have shops back in Leeds, don't you?" Diana replied.

"We're from Pudsey," said someone near the back.

"Good for you" said Diana. "We're going down Oxford Street later and, yes, there are plenty of shops. London has so much to offer that it's impossible to absorb it all in a short time. But believe me when I say that your tour will give you a thorough and absorbing glimpse into a world that impacts upon every single one of us."

There were snorts of derision. It might not have been the trip the group wanted, but Diana would make sure their visit to the Palace of Westminster was memorable.

## Chapter Two

Newton drove on, past leafy Hyde Park and on into Belgravia. Ornate Georgian facades flanked the roads.

Diana angled the microphone towards Zaf. She could talk all day about London and never get bored. But Zaf had been with the company less than a month, and she wanted to let him work on his tour guide skills. And it looked like he could do with a distraction from whatever had happened with Malachi.

They switched places and Diana moved down the bus.

"You'll want to see this," Zaf said into the mic. "Over that wall is Buckingham Palace."

They all turned to look at the high wall.

"The bricks here in London are that pale colour," said Zaf. "Reminds me of Hobnobs."

"We can't see over it, though," someone complained.

Zaf shrugged. "I know. To be fair, though, if I was King Charles, I'd have a massive wall too. He wants to barbecue his organic sausages without us watching."

There were laughs and groans. Diana knew that groans

were just good as laughs in this business. It was engagement, and that was what counted.

"Now, has anyone spotted the famous clock tower?" asked Zaf. "We're nearly there."

Through the trees along Millbank, Diana could see the looming tower of Big Ben, an iconic work of neo-Gothic architecture. "Big Ben, properly known as the Elizabeth Tower, is ninety-six metres tall," said Zaf. "It's one of the tallest clock towers in the country. The tallest freestanding clock tower, that's Old Joe in my manor: Birmingham." He smiled, despite the fact that the students were ignoring him. "But Big Ben is... what's this?"

They all craned their necks as the bus turned left into Parliament Square, Westminster Abbey on the left and the open space of the square on the right. There was a crowd of protestors on the grass. Placards jostled for attention and music boomed out.

"Is it a riot?" asked one boy.

"Of course not." Diana stood up from her position at the back of the bus. "They're just exercising their right to protest. It looks like an anti-poverty rally. There might be a news crew or two somewhere."

Zaf pointed to a placard bearing four words. "Does that one say, *No More Fat Cats* or *No Fat More Cats*?" He turned to the group. "Sounds like a rule to live your life by. No fat, more cats. Stick it on a T-shirt."

No one laughed.

The bus pulled up at the drop off point.

"You can leave a bag on the bus," called Zaf, "but food or rubbish'll be binned. Newton likes to keep things neat and tidy."

He did a sweep of the upper deck while Diana herded everyone off.

"See you later, Newton!" she called.

Newton gave them a wave. He'd waste no time getting out his special cloths and polishing every last smudge off the vintage chrome while the group was away.

Zaf followed the last student off the bus. Diana leaned over to him. "I'm so sorry to hear about you and Malachi."

"It's already forgotten." Zaf shook his head. "He'd told me he wasn't sure what he wanted from life. Turns out he knew what he *didn't* want. It was amicable, kinda, but there were a few words on my way out the door."

Diana patted his arm. "Good for you. Why not come over to mine for tea and cake some time and tell me all about it?"

"An invitation to the woman's boudoir." Zaf waggled his sculpted eyebrows. "That'll set tongues wagging."

The two teachers approached Diana.

"Seems you've got everything here under control," said Mrs Swinburne. "We can meet you back at the hotel later."

"I beg your pardon?" Diana replied.

"We're needed elsewhere." Mr Chaplin fiddled with the zip of his coat.

"Your entire group is here," Diana pointed out.

"Important admin," said Mr Chaplin. He passed her a stapled bundle of papers. "Here's the risk assessment. It's got our numbers on it."

"I hope your sudden and urgent admin isn't too *onerous*."

"Also, how do we get to Hamleys from here?" asked Mrs Swinburne.

"It's um, near to the place where we're needed," added Chaplin.

"It's on Regent Street." Diana's jaw was clenched. "I'm

sure you can work it out, what with you being teachers and everything. It's walkable from here."

They scuttled off, consulting their phones for directions.

"They're having an affair," Ava whispered to Diana.

"Is that so?" Diana forced a smile and raised her voice. "Right, everyone. We're heading round to the Cromwell Green entrance. We need to stay together. Follow me!" She lifted her brolly high.

Yes, a brightly coloured umbrella was a tour guide cliché, but in a city where the weather could change minute by minute, it was also practical. Diana had found it at a market in Brick Lane and enjoyed the whimsy of its duck-head handle. And if the duck head, along with the old-fashioned nature of the Chartwell and Crouch uniform, gave her a certain Mary Poppins vibe, then that was no bad thing.

"Are we going to see where Guy Fawkes got killed?" Ethan shouted out.

"He was arrested here, Ethan," Diana called back. "Not killed. No one gets killed in the Houses of Parliament."

# Chapter Three

Diana spoke to the group from the front while Zaf checked no one had been left behind.

"Now it looks like Zaf and I will be steering you through your day. So I'd be grateful for your patience and co-operation. Let's head to the entrance."

"Or we could go to Hamleys," said Ethan.

"Why don't you just go then?" snapped Ava. "Some of us want to be here. It'd be better without you."

Zaf resisted a laugh. He wasn't much older than this lot, and he could see his younger self in a few of them.

But Diana wasn't taking any nonsense. "Hamleys is for children, Ethan. You can do better than that." She raised her voice to speak to the group. "Don't forget I've got an attendance register for your school records, to prove that you all attended each part of the trip."

Zaf knew that was a lie. But he'd watched Diana in action for a few weeks now, and knew better than to point that out.

"Keep up," she told the group. "We need to clear security."

The queue at the Cromwell Green entrance was short and

they were soon inside the security hall. Zaf brought up the rear, checking that everyone had got through.

"It's like an airport," said one of the girls.

"They don't want people to bring in weapons, moron," said another.

"Morning, Gillian." Diana exchanged smiles with a tall security guard who gave a friendly nod as she returned her brolly. Zaf sometimes thought Diana knew half of London.

Once everyone was through the body scanners and had picked up their bags and coats, Diana led them into Westminster Hall. Zaf shuffled in at the back as she turned to smile at them.

"Welcome inside! Take a look at this incredible room. It's the oldest part of the estate. William the Conqueror's son, William Rufus, commissioned this building in 1097, making it over nine hundred years old."

Most of the students ignored Diana, a few posing for grinning selfies instead. Ava stared up at the ceiling. She looked like she was about to ask a question about the roof, but then she frowned. "Are we meeting John Chapman-Moore now?"

Zaf had no idea who his MP had been at any point in his life. Maybe Chapman-Moore had visited the school to promote the project.

"In a moment we'll be going through to the Central Lobby," said Diana, "where we'll meet Mr Chapman-Moore. We will pass through a couple of fascinating rooms, and you'll get the chance to admire them. We can take photographs here and in the next two rooms, but once we're in Central Lobby you'll need to put your phones away."

Zaf realised the teacher's pet was looking at him.

"Everything OK?" he asked her.

"So what happened with you and your boyfriend?" Ava replied.

Zaf blinked. "I'm not talking about the boyfriend thing. It's very raw." He cast about for distractions. "Look! I spy something insta-worthy." He pointed ahead up the stairs. "Who wants to take a picture of me with laughing-boy here?"

He hurried up to a gold statue of a heraldic beast and posed beside it. "It's like a cheeky dragon, or maybe a winged cat that's had too much catnip."

"It's an evil clown with wings," one of the group said.

"Nah, it's a demon."

"It's an eagle if you got it from Wish."

"Maybe they didn't know what dragons looked like then cos they didn't have photos," said Ethan.

"That's wise, Ethan." Zaf grinned.

The group laughed as Zaf imitated the open-mouthed gape of the statue. They took pictures, then tried it for themselves. Diana winked at Zaf and he smiled back.

They carried on through St Stephen's Hall. The far door was held open by a pair of cleaners polishing the brass fittings, and the air was heavy with the tang of brass-cleaner. Zaf had done several tours of Parliament and the smell was always the same: brass, leather and ancient dust.

"This is the last place where you can take photos," warned Diana.

The group went on a picture-taking frenzy while Zaf gazed up at the enormous pictures on the walls.

"Zaf's university degree is in Art History," Diana said, "so we could challenge him to tell us about these paintings."

"Or even more of a challenge," he replied, "we could try spotting a black or brown person in any of them."

"Or a woman," said Ava.

Zaf held out a fist for her to bump.

They came into the circular room that was Central Lobby. People hurried back and forth, meeting colleagues and constituents and passing between other parts of the building.

"So do they do, like, rituals in here?" Ethan pointed at the floor. "It's got that star thing marked out, for making sacrifices."

Zaf shook his head. "I wasn't the best at maths, but I have seen more than my fair share of horror, so I'd suggest you check the number of points." He stepped over to the emblem. "How many points?"

"Eight," someone shouted.

"Bang on," said Zaf. "If you've watched horror films, you'll know ritualistic slaughter takes place in a *five*-pointed star. It's like the law or something." He smiled. "I hope that clears things up." He looked at Ethan. "No ritual sacrifices, sorry mate."

# Chapter Four

Diana scanned the central lobby for John Chapman-Moore. His official picture on the Houses of Parliament website had shown a fleshy, balding man of around sixty, but she couldn't see anyone like that here.

She checked the clock by the central lobby post office: ten o'clock. The MP was late. Zaf was hovering at the back of the tour group, rubbing his eyes.

A man in a grey suit with lined cheeks and grey mutton-chop whiskers ambled up to her.

"Simon." She smiled.

"Diana Bakewell, what are you doing here?"

She gestured at the group around her and he nodded in understanding.

"You stiffening for us any time soon?" he asked

"Do you need me?"

"This Rachmaninoff is besting us. I can put a word in with the alto baronesses."

"Maybe," she replied.

Simon shrugged and moved on.

Zaf leaned in to Diana. "Stiffening?"

"Stiffening. It's—"

"Miss, how come they get their own post office?" a student interrupted.

"Don't forget that a huge number of people work here," Diana told her.

"Yeah, but why can't they use WhatsApp like everyone else?"

"That would be a good question to ask Mr Chapman-Moore. Has anyone here met him before?"

The students shook their heads.

"My mum wrote and asked him to open the school fun day, but he said he was too busy," said one girl. "He sent a box of chocolate liqueurs for the tombola instead."

"My mum used to work for him," began another, as a ginger-haired twenty-something woman in a smart jacket and skirt appeared beside Diana.

"This must be the party from Foxwood Grange," said the woman.

"It is." Diana held out a hand. "I'm Diana Bakewell, their tour guide."

"Florence Breecher." She shook Diana's hand. "I'm John's researcher."

"No Mr Chapman-Moore today?"

"I'll take you to his office."

"Ah." Diana pushed down her irritation. "Keep up, everyone!"

Diana corralled the group as Florence led them through the corridors. As well as the functionaries, office employees and support workers, there were security guards dotted about, as well as a smaller number of police officers. Florence stopped at a security desk and had everyone issued with temporary passes on lanyards.

They passed through into the less public spaces. "This place is huge," said one of the students when they reached their third tiled corridor.

"The Palace of Westminster covers eight acres of land," said Diana. "That's about four football pitches. There are one thousand one hundred rooms, a hundred staircases and nearly three miles of corridor."

"No wonder I'm so worn out all the time." Florence smiled, but there was a frazzled tone to her voice.

"Long days, huh?" asked Ethan.

"Oh, I love the job," Florence said. "I got the role after being an intern. It's hard work though, so relaxing doesn't come easy. I like to work hard and play hard, as they say."

"The lady likes to party!" crowed Ethan. "You can show us some nightlife, maybe?"

Florence said nothing.

"What about the expense of living in London?" asked Zaf. "Does a researcher's job pay enough for that?"

Florence made a *so-so* gesture with her hand. "I share a flat with my cousin Tabitha. She works here too. Any kind of space here in London is at a premium, but Tabitha and I rub along fine. She's just flunked her exams so I'm putting on a bit of a party for her tomorrow night, take her mind off things."

The group emitted rumbles of sympathy for exam-based evils.

Up ahead were two figures. One, paler, fleshier and older than his official photo, was clearly John Chapman-Moore MP. The other was a severe-featured and dark-haired woman in a black eighteenth-century coat and a high white collar: the

Serjeant at Arms. She leaned on a curved-handled walking stick as she stood there.

"Doors and rooms, John. Doors and rooms," the woman was saying as a cleaner squeezed past them. "If you want your numbers to add up then you need to—"

She turned as the tour party approached, gave Chapman-Moore a curt nod, and departed with an uneven gait, her buckled patent leather shoes and the tip of her walking stick clicking on the tiles.

The bald MP turned to the approaching group.

"Ah, good morning," he said in a deep and sonorous voice. "You must be the group from Pudsey."

"These are the students from Foxwood Grange Academy," Florence told him.

"Of course. My constituents and future voters. I am John Chapman-Moore, independent MP for Pudsey and Otley."

Chapman-Moore went round the group shaking each person's hand, greeting them and asking names.

When Ethan introduced himself as 'Tiger' the group burst out laughing, but Chapman-Moore was unfazed. As he passed Diana, she noticed his gaze slide straight off her. Ava, last to have her hand shaken, seemed cool as she greeted him. *Not a future Chapman-Moore voter*, Diana thought.

"Come in and see my office," said the MP, "and I'll talk you through some of the things I do in the course of a normal working day. Of course, this is very much a refreshing break from the normal working day for me. I'm delighted to see youngsters so keen on politics. Can't wait to pour knowledge and experience into those eager young brains of yours."

Diana saw Zaf grimace, but she smiled politely.

"Come in, come in." Chapman-Moore led the group into

the office. "Get right in. Ignore my fellow MP Azar there. Budge up. Everyone in. Tight squeeze."

The wood-panelled office was grand, but struggled to contain twenty-odd teenagers, even standing. Chapman-Moore looked over the heads of the students at Diana and Zaf. "Tour guides can wait outside."

The last of the students squeezed in, and a bespectacled man in a suit pushed his way out into the corridor and shut the door behind him. He gave Diana a half-amused, half-exasperated look.

"Azar Mirza MP," he said. "I've apparently been banished from my own shared office by Mr Chapman-Moore and a bunch of kids from Yorkshire. Still, it beats having a tiny basement office somewhere." He gave her another exasperated look and walked away.

The conversation inside was a muffled mumble.

"An independent MP?" asked Zaf.

"Chapman Moore isn't a member of a political party," she replied.

Zaf had his phone out and was scrolling. "I get it. He was a Tory MP for ten years and then he had 'the whip' removed. Er...?"

"It doesn't mean what you think."

# Chapter Five

Zaf continued scrolling. "You can even see how MPs voted on things," he told Diana. "Property owner occupation, fire safety bills, commercial rent. Jeez, MPs debate a lot of boring things."

"Boring or not," Diana said, "the lifeblood of government flows through here."

The office door opened and the students all but exploded into the corridor. Florence the researcher was at the front of the tide. Zaf shifted aside, only just getting out of the way in time.

"On to the Members' Lobby," announced Florence, "and we'll see John again in the Commons Chamber."

There was muttering among the students about how boring the last ten minutes had been.

"He goes on worse than Mr Finch in History," said one.

"Do all MPs have offices like that?" a boy asked.

"There are six hundred and fifty MPs," said Florence. "They all have an office, spread around this building and Portcullis House, over the road. Not everyone has such a nice office as Mr Chapman-Moore."

"Did you see his coffee maker?" Ethan said. "Top of the range bean-to-cup machine."

"I can't believe you kept asking him about his coffee maker," Ava muttered.

"It cost a thousand quid. How could I not be interested?"

Florence nodded. "I put together the business case that demonstrated it was a worthwhile investment. If you stack up the time and money a busy MP can save if he's not queuing up for takeaway coffee..."

"Would he be the one queuing up, or would he send you to do it?" asked a girl.

"Anyway, my questions were better than yours," Ethan was telling Ava. "What rubbish were you asking? *What did you do before you were an MP? Who did you work with?* You are a tedious human being, Ava Franks."

Zaf spotted Ava cradling a hand inside her jacket, her face tight.

"You OK?" he asked.

"What?" she snapped. "Yeah, yeah, yeah. Fine."

Florence was throwing herself into the role of tour guide, letting Zaf and Diana take on a shepherding role.

"We'll spend a few minutes in the Members' Lobby," she said, "where you might recognise some statues and busts of former prime ministers. Take a look around."

In contrast to the wood panelling elsewhere, this room was decorated with intricately carved stone, stretching above them in elegant arches.

Ethan stood under an arch. "Look, I'm being told off by Finch and Chaplin."

Zaf had to smile. The statues on either side of the arch were of politicians in action. They did look a bit like teachers telling someone off.

"That's Thatcher." A young man pointed at a statue. "My dad said she were a witch or summat."

"She was Prime Minister for eleven years," said Florence. "Not quite as famous as the man on the other side, there. Anyone know who that is?"

"It's that one out of *Doctor Who*," said someone.

"Boris Johnson without his wig on," said someone else.

"It's Winston Churchill." Ava tutted.

"Correct," said Florence. "I think it's too soon to see Mr Johnson here. It used to be that prime ministers had to be dead for ten years before they could have their sculpture here, but that rule's been relaxed."

"I heard that it's illegal to die in here," said Ethan. "Like if one of us dropped dead right now, we'd be breaking the law."

Ava looked at Ethan. "Even by your standards that's stupid."

Ethan rounded on her. "My dad heard it in a pub quiz so it's definitely true."

Diana raised a hand. "The argument is that anyone who dies here is entitled to a state funeral, so they made it illegal to die here. But I'm afraid it's just an urban myth."

"Anyway," Florence said. "We'll be going into the House of Commons in a moment. The House of Lords is down there, the second chamber which holds the Commons to account. They each have their own debating space: green seating means we're in the Commons, red is the Lords."

"Lovely overview, Florence," said Diana.

"I should tell you about the *Helping Hands for Homeless* bill. It's John's brainchild, we're very passionate about it. We want to see homelessness properly addressed, so it's a proposal for accommodation to be made available to people affected by it. It offers tax breaks and packages of financial support to make it happen."

"Sounds good," said Zaf.

"The pilot project has been running for a year," Florence continued, "but the vote next week will roll it out across the country. You'll hear more about it from John in a few minutes. Let's move into the Chamber, shall we?"

The students, bored by talk of parliamentary bills and homelessness, trudged after her.

"Just so you know," Ethan said to Zaf, "the only reason I've not died of boredom right now is because of it being illegal."

"Urban myth," Zaf reminded him.

"Oh, yeah. Then prepare to have a bored corpse on your hands, mate."

## Chapter Six

The Foxwood Grange group followed Florence Breecher into the House of Commons Chamber, a curious space to Diana's mind. It was as rich in wooden carvings and historic detail as a church, but the seating was just utilitarian benches. The public gallery overhead was shielded by a transparent screen.

There was no debate taking place now and tourists were spread across the chamber. They filtered in from behind the Speaker's chair and past the rows of seating.

Florence encouraged the students to go up into the seats and explore. A cleaner moved aside to let them pass just as John Chapman-Moore bustled in. He clapped his hands to get their attention.

"Hello and welcome to my wonderful group of young people! Had business to deal with back there. I hope that my darling researcher has been looking after you in my absence."

"Darling?" sniggered one of the boys.

Chapman-Moore seemed not to hear. "Now, we've got so

much to talk about, lots of ground to cover. How about a little quiz to see how much you know about modern day politics?"

Diana caught the panicked faces of the students.

"I'll start with an easy one. What is the name of the—"

Chapman-Moore's words were cut short by a scream.

A young woman wearing a beanie ran across the floor. She dropped the bag she'd been carrying and pulled something from a pocket.

Diana froze, staring. A little voice inside her was saying, *Do something. Do something.* But she couldn't move.

There were shouts from the students and other tourists.

*"What's she doing?"*

*"Is that a gun?"*

*"Get down!"*

The screaming woman tugged at the object in her hand and flung it at John Chapman-Moore.

"No more fat cats!" she yelled. "No more!"

An explosive splatter hit the chamber seats.

It was paint, white paint. The white was shocking against the aged oak and the sober green leather of the benches. Confused and upset shouts came from the students.

Zaf had his arms out, as though trying to wrap the students in a protective hug. The students at floor level were stumbling away.

A team of security guards swooped in. They wrestled the empty pot from the woman's hand and dragged her to the ground.

The guards clustered around Chapman-Moore. Diana couldn't tell if he'd been hit by the paint.

She swept the area and performed the quickest tour group head count of her life. *Eighteen, nineteen, twenty...*

As her gaze fell on Ava, she spotted the young woman on the floor behind her. First the feet, then the legs.

Florence Breecher had fallen. But she wasn't moving to get up.

Diana pushed forward.

Parliament security bundled the spluttering and confused MP out of the chamber. Two more dragged the paint-flinging protestor away.

Ava turned as Diana rushed past her. "Oh my God," the girl said.

Florence was on the floor, twisted onto her side. Her jacket was dark and slick with blood.

Sticking out of her back was the glinting metal handle of a knife.

"Someone's hurt!" came a shout.

Diana knelt down by the researcher. "Florence! Florence, can you hear me?"

Ava was beside her, saying something Diana couldn't hear over the cacophony of voices. Ava's hand wrapped around the blade handle to pull it out.

"No," said Diana.

She took hold of the blade as she slid Ava's hands away. "Put pressure on the wound." She placed Ava's flat palms on the area around the injury. "Keep the pressure on."

Diana looked up and raised her voice. "Help, somebody! This woman is hurt!"

She grabbed Florence's wrist, two fingers placed to feel for a pulse.

Nothing.

Why was no one coming to help? Hadn't she been loud enough?

"Some help over here please! First aid!" she heard Zaf shout.

A young security guard appeared on Florence's other side. He spoke into a walkie talkie. "Need first aid in the House of Commons. A woman has been stabbed."

"She's not breathing," Diana heard herself say.

"Victim is unresponsive," the guard said into his radio.

Ava looked up at Diana, wild panic in her eyes. Zaf was there now, gentle hands levering the student away. He lifted Ava up as a pair of emergency first aiders ran in to take over. Diana pulled away and stepped back.

The rest of the students were clustered high up on the seating to one side. They held onto one another, staring.

Diana had to go to them. They were her responsibility.

She looked back at the injured woman.

In that brief glance, she saw many things.

She saw Florence Breecher with the brass handle of a knife sticking out of her back, the splatter of white paint in a line across the floor and over the tops of the benches.

She saw her own umbrella, dropped in her haste to help Florence.

She saw more security guards rushing in, including the dark-haired Serjeant at Arms stepping in from behind the Commons Speaker's chair.

But the one thing that drew Diana's attention more than anything else was a white coffee cup resting on the floor, less than an arm's length from Florence's body. A white ceramic coffee cup.

Sitting on the floor of the House of Commons, where it had no right to be.

# Chapter Seven

If Zaf hadn't been in charge of two dozen shocked and upset sixth form students, he might have burst into tears.

He wasn't afraid to show emotion. But the situation had brought out some weird mother hen instinct in him, and the only way he could cope was by clinging onto his role as tour guide.

As the Parliament security guard guided everyone out of the Chamber and down the corridor to the Robing Room beyond the Lords' Chamber, Zaf kept the group together. He placed a hand on a shuddering shoulder here and offered words of encouragement there.

Diana was with them, but seemed either shocked or lost in thought.

She caught Zaf's gaze. "The register."

"They're all here." Zaf did another recount.

The Robing Room was a mostly unfurnished, blue-carpeted room, currently being used as a holding space for thirty-odd people.

Seeing the blood on Diana's hands, Zaf passed her a packet of wipes, then offered one to Ava.

Diana, who seemed to be finding herself again, gathered the students in a corner and had them sit down.

"This is like a primary school assembly, isn't it?" said Zaf, fighting against the flow of emotions to inject a lighter note into the situation.

"What?" said a boy.

"You know, all cross-legged on the floor. I should say *Good morning, boys and girls* and then you'll say, *Good morning, Mr Williams* and then we'll have a nice policeman come in and do a talk about road safety."

There were heads shaking. Groans, too. But what was it Diana said? Groans were as good as laughs in this business.

"We've all had a terrible shock." Diana cleared her throat. "And we have every right to be upset. But you need to know that we are safe here. We're all together and we're safe."

She reached inside her jacket and took out the crumpled risk assessment sheet the teachers had left with her.

Zaf stared at it. "I don't think murders will be on the school risk assessment."

"The teachers' numbers," Diana snapped. "Message them."

Zaf flicked through the sheets, listening as Diana spoke to the students.

"While we're here, we might as well continue the tour," she said.

"Really, Miss?"

"It'll keep my mind occupied, and hopefully yours, too." She swept an arm towards the dais at the far end of the room. A trio of shell-shocked tourists sat on the steps. "As you might guess, that is where the monarch sits, and this is the room where they put on their crown and robes before entering the

Lords. The room is filled with imagery associated with chivalry and bravery. St George there. St Michael."

"George Michael?" asked a girl.

Zaf watched as Diana forced a smile.

"No," she said. "The lack of a statue to George Michael is clearly an oversight and will hopefully be rectified as soon as possible. But what I love most in here are the frescoes and wood carvings showing the life of King Arthur. Does anyone know the story?"

Now she had the attention of most of the other tourists in the room, as well as the young people. It was comforting to listen to a confident, knowledgeable voice. Zaf felt his heart rate steady.

"Right. If we look up, we can see King Arthur in his court as Sir Tristram arrives. This is a representation of the virtue of hospitality…"

Zaf had found the right page in the risk assessment. T Chaplin and J Swinburne. He took out his phone.

A police officer appeared at his elbow. Not Parliament security, but an actual copper like his sister Connie. Hi-vis jacket and everything.

"Who are you calling?" the PC asked.

"Their teachers." Zaf indicated the students.

"You can't make phone calls."

"Someone needs to tell their teachers, before their families find out another way."

Half the students had their phones in their hands. Were they messaging? Were they instagramming?

"You need to get them off their phones," said the copper.

Zaf could have laughed. "Have you tried separating teenagers from their devices?"

A hulking figure appeared in the doorway, a folded trench coat slung over his thick arm.

"Names and ID off everyone," he instructed an officer near him. "And we'll take initial statements." His gaze rested on Zaf. "I'm Detective Chief Inspector Clint Sugarbrook, and I think we'll start with you, sir."

## Chapter Eight

"And in this final one," said Diana, drawing the whole room's attention to the final mahogany carving on the wall of the Robing Room, "we see the death of King Arthur."

"*Sir Mordred slaine. King Arthur wounded to death.*" One of the students read the gold painted title beneath.

"Who's Mordred?" asked a boy.

"He is said to be King Arthur's nephew who, jealous of Arthur, tried to usurp his throne."

"So why's Arthur reaching out to him?" asked Ethan.

Diana considered the carving. She'd always thought that Arthur's outstretched hand was just flopping.

She suddenly pictured Florence's body, limp and sprawled on the Commons floor.

*Focus.* She had a job to do.

She cleared her throat. "Enemies or not, Arthur perhaps still loved Mordred. Even after they had destroyed each other, there might have been love there."

The double doors to the left of the dais opened, and the giant police detective, DCI Sugarbrook, re-entered with Zaf.

"Diana Bakewell?" he said.

She lifted her chin. "I'm Diana."

"I need a word with—"

"I need a word with you too." Half an hour holed up in this space had given her time to think.

The huge man turned on his heels and marched off, assuming she would follow.

Diana did, but at her own pace.

"OK," she heard Zaf say to the students, slipping back into his role. "I'm giving top points for whoever can tell me which celebrities these guys in the pictures look like. And why aren't there any pictures of Merlin the wizard, huh?"

Sugarbrook led Diana off to the side, through a corridor with dark wood-panelled walls then past a pair of uniformed police officers and into a nondescript office.

A dark-haired woman was squashed up at one end of the desk with a notepad and laptop.

"Ah, DS Quigley," Sugarbrook said. He turned to Diana. "Do you have any ID on you, Madam?"

Diana dipped into her pocket, scrutinising his wide face, and took out her slim work purse. He inspected her photo driving licence.

"This is fifteen years out of date."

"It's still me," she said. "You're related to Joe Sugarbrook, are you?"

The man's heavy eyebrows descended in a frown. "My father."

Diana nodded. "I saw 'Samoan Joe' Sugarbrook box against the Shadwell Shadow at York Hall in Bethnal Green in…" She sucked in as she tried to recall. "… nineteen eighty-nine."

The DCI regarded her with surprise. "He wasn't actually Samoan, you know? He was from the Solomon Islands."

"I guess it didn't have the same ring," she said.

He eyed her. "You knew him?"

She shook her head. "I went with my own dad to that fight. A heavyweight match. I have a good memory for people and faces."

He gave her the tiniest nod.

"Miss Diana Bakewell, good with people and faces, do you know John Chapman-Moore?"

"I met him for the first time today."

"Do you know the woman who attacked him?"

"Attacked him...?" She frowned. "The paint woman? No. Was she with the anti-poverty protestors in Parliament Square?"

The other officer, DS Quigley, made a note in her pad.

"And did you see the person who stabbed Florence Breecher?" Sugarbrook asked.

"I did not. We were all distracted. She's dead, isn't she?"

"I'm afraid so," said Sugarbrook. "Do you know anyone who would wish Mr Chapman-Moore harm?"

"Chapman-Moore?"

"We are dealing with a real and possibly time-sensitive threat to our MPs. Any clues you can give us would be useful."

It was Diana's turn to frown. "Florence was the victim, Inspector. Florence."

He gave a small grunt.

Diana stared at him. Florence, alive or dead, was clearly not his priority.

He whispered to his colleague, who turned the laptop round and brought up an image. It was the murder weapon, a narrow blood-smeared blade photographed as it lay on the

Commons floor. From point to handle, it was a lustrous bronze colour.

"Someone took a great deal of effort to sneak this weapon into the Commons," the DCI said. "Did you touch it when attending to Miss Breecher's injuries?"

"I did. Myself and one of my party. Ava..." Diana reached for a surname. "Franks. We tried to administer first aid."

"Possibly obliterating any fingerprints on the handle."

"We were trying to save her life."

Sugarbrook said nothing.

Diana felt anger rise within her. "You are going to try to find her killer, aren't you?"

"That's exactly why we're here."

"She was young and enthusiastic," said Diana. "She was filled with passion for her job. Probably burning the candle at both ends. Work hard, play hard, she said. She believed in the laws she helped bring into effect."

"You knew her personally?" asked Sugarbrook.

"No, Chief Inspector." Diana didn't disguise the anger in her voice. "I took the time to get to know her. All you have to do is listen. And look."

He nodded, unfazed. "You're upset. Would you like a tissue?"

*Do I look like I need a tissue?*

"I'm fine." Diana's voice shook.

"Good. I'll need to talk to this Ava Franks."

Diana sat up. "I'm going to make a suggestion, Detective Chief Inspector. More than a suggestion. There are twenty-two young people sat in the Robing Room. And if I know young people, they're probably already asking to go to the loo and wanting to know what's for lunch."

"I appreciate it's inconvenient —"

"And we're all part of a single tour group, staying at the Redhouse Hotel on Chiltern Street. You know it?"

He hesitated.

"I don't think you suspect a bunch of school students from Leeds of planning to bring a knife through Parliament security checks," she said. "And as for actually managing the feat..."

She stared meaningfully at him.

"No, no, of course."

Diana took the crumpled school risk assessment from inside her jacket. "The names are on there. You can let us go now. Perhaps you can interview some of them at your leisure later on."

He began to speak, but was interrupted by the door opening and the Serjeant at Arms entering.

"Detective," the woman said, walking stick gripped tightly, "I have members who want to know when they can return to their offices."

"Miss O'Grady—" Sugarbrook began.

"Let me rephrase," she said. "I shall permit the members to pass through the lobby to their offices. I understand that the Commons Chamber remains a crime scene for now."

Diana knew that the Serjeant at Arms, despite the stuffy title and the even stuffier uniform, was a post that wielded real power. Who was in charge here, her or the police?

Sugarbrook gave the Serjeant at Arms a curt nod and she withdrew.

"Miss Bakewell," he said. "I'll ask for you and your party to be escorted out as soon as it's safe. We will speak again."

He stood. Diana stood too.

"Thanks for your time," he said.

"I dropped my umbrella in the Commons chamber," she said. "I'd like it back. It has a duck's head."

"Donald or Daffy?" said Sugarbrook.

"I always thought he looked more like a Reginald." She paused at the door. "And there was the cup."

"What cup?"

"The white coffee cup. An ordinary cup. On the floor next to Florence's body. That wasn't mine. It was just there."

He frowned. "I don't see the relevance."

"Nor do I," said Diana. "Not yet."

## Chapter Nine

Diana returned to the Robing Room to find Zaf on the phone, attempting to explain what had happened to Newton Crombie. He had the call on speakerphone and the students were listening, keen to know when they were going to leave.

"We're shut in the Robing Room," said Zaf. "The police won't let us go. No idea how long it'll be."

He put a hand over the phone. "Newton's outside," he whispered. "He's trying to get to us."

Diana nodded.

"The police keep trying to move me on," said Newton from the other end of the line. "Saying they're clearing the area. There's no consideration at all. None."

Zaf looked up at Diana.

"We're leaving now," she said, loud enough for Newton to hear.

"Brilliant. Hear that?" Zaf hung up.

With grunts, groans and yawns, the students of Foxwood Grange pulled themselves up from the floor.

"Are we carrying on with the tour?" one asked.

"It's straight back to the hotel for now," Diana replied. "You need rest."

"Before heading out to the clubs and bars," suggested Ethan.

"We're going to the gift shop before we go though, aren't we?" asked a girl.

"Sorry?" said Diana.

"They've got a gift shop. It says on the website."

Diana stared at the students. She spotted a smile flickering on Zaf's lips. All the upsets of the morning and still they wanted to spend their money on overpriced souvenirs.

"With me." She led them out of the Robing Room and back in the direction of Westminster Hall.

The huge space of Westminster Hall was now empty of tourists. Instead, it was dotted with Parliament security and Metropolitan Police officers. Off to one side a door led through to the gift shop, café and exit.

The students were happy to distract themselves with Houses of Parliament memorabilia.

"Incredible," Diana said.

Zaf leaned in and whispered, "I thought they'd be too distressed, but seriously. A gift shop is the answer to everything."

Diana watched the students sift through all the options, comparing products and prices and generally demonstrating more concentration than they'd shown all day.

"I don't understand the socks," Ethan told the rest of the group.

"*Ayes to the right, noes to the left*. It's about voting," said a girl. "Anyway, you should think about the bodywash if you ask me."

"Nobody *did* ask you," Ethan replied. "Hey, d'you think the gunpowder mustard's got real gunpowder in it?"

Diana shook her head and gave Zaf a smile. "The Guy Fawkes range. Stay classy, Palace of Westminster."

She squeezed past two policemen who seemed to be contemplating buying a bottle of Houses of Parliament red wine and went through to the café. It would be a good holding point before they went out to the bus.

As she entered, a young woman jumped up from a table and approached her.

"You're with the tour group, aren't you?" The woman looked dishevelled, her eyes red-rimmed and her cheeks stained with tears. "I keep getting blocked from going back into that part of the building."

"Are you alright?" asked Diana.

"I'm Tabitha Welkin—"

"Florence's cousin." The woman shared her cousin's coppery ginger hair. "The flatmate."

"I got a call saying she's dead, but that can't be right. I'm her emergency contact, but nobody wants to talk to me, and I don't know what I'm supposed to do. You were the group she was with when..."

"I'm so very sorry for your loss, Tabitha." Diana clasped the woman's hands.

"It's true, then?" Tabitha pulled her hands away. She swallowed hard to stifle a sob, then frowned. "Wait, there's blood on you."

Diana looked down. Dried blood stained the cuffs of her blouse. "I carried out some first aid."

Tabitha put a hand to her mouth and sobbed.

"Hey." Diana drew her into a hug. In among that pervasive

Westminster Palace smell – leather, brass and dust – she could now detect the iron tang of blood.

"What do I even do?" Tabitha sobbed. "What do you do when someone dies?"

"Shhh..."

"Am I supposed to go somewhere and... and..." Tabitha pulled back, flapping a hand.

"You don't need to do anything at all, not today." Diana clasped the woman's shoulder. "I'm Diana. Chartwell and Crouch tours. Your cousin told us about you today. With such fondness."

"Really?"

Diana gave her a sad smile. "She was going to throw a party for you."

"I know. I know." With difficulty, Tabitha pulled her face into a tight smile. "A party was her answer to everything. Such life."

Diana nodded. "Today will be hard, Tabitha. Impossibly hard. But it will end and then there will be tomorrow and the next day. It gets easier."

There was a burst of laughter as the first of the Foxwood Grange students exited the gift shop. Young Ethan had indeed bought a pair of novelty socks.

Diana turned back to Tabitha, who seemed to have found her composure.

"You're busy." Tabitha began to back away.

"I'm happy to talk. Anytime."

Tabitha mouthed a *thank you* and retreated as the students poured out with such energy that it seemed impossible to believe they had just witnessed the aftermath of a murder.

## Chapter Ten

The Redhouse Hotel was at one end of Chiltern Street in Marylebone, with the Chartwell and Crouch bus depot further down the other side, not far from Baker Street. The proximity of the bus company to its favoured hotel was useful, especially when it came to dropping off guests at the end of a long day.

As the students trooped off the bus, Zaf exchanged a glance with Diana. "Shall I go and get them settled in? I can see you back at the depot in a few minutes, save you waiting."

Diana nodded. "Thanks, Zaf, that sounds good. And... ah! There are words I need to have with these two."

Zaf followed her gaze and saw the teachers, Chaplin and Swinburne, hurrying up the street. They had the decency to look red-faced with concern (and exertion), but both carried bulging shopping bags.

"Mr Chaplin, Miss Swinburne." Diana's voice was stern. She'd have made a good teacher, Zaf thought.

*Best to get the students out of the way.*

Zaf held his arms wide to herd the stragglers into the hotel reception. As he did so, Newton pulled away with a wave. Their driver would be keen to *put the bus to bed*, as he called it.

In reception, Zaf found the guest liaison manager behind the reception desk. "Penny, your guests are ready for some liaising."

"Is that so?" said Penny with a wry smile.

Penny Slipper was only a few years older than Zaf, but she gave off the impression of someone who'd got her life together. It was reinforced by the smart waistcoat and shirt the Redhouse Hotel staff wore. But she always made Zaf feel uneasy.

"They had an eventful time at the Houses of Parliament," he told her.

"Did you get caught up in that stabbing business? It's been all over the news."

Zaf nodded. "Diana got them out of there, but the police still want to talk to them. They witnessed the whole thing."

"No!" Penny turned to the students still gathered in reception. "I'm sorry to hear you've all had such a dreadful day. We've got your group table in the dining room ready, so we'll give you thirty minutes to freshen up, and then you can come down for your evening meal."

Ethan puffed out his cheeks, exhaled loudly and looked at Zaf. "I need to blow off some steam after today. I might skip dinner and go out."

Ava rolled her eyes at him. "What are you on about, Ethan? You just stood there. Some of us at least tried to help."

Zaf looked at the blood stains, still there on the cuffs of Ava's blouse. *Tough kid.*

"Your meals are included in the price of your stay," said Penny. "Entertainment has been organised."

"I expect your teachers'll want to catch up with you," said

Zaf, "and make sure you're doing OK." He didn't mention that the police would probably be dropping by, too. "Er, what is tonight's entertainment?"

Penny checked a sheet. "A politics themed quiz," she replied with unconvincing enthusiasm. "There's prizes."

Ethan stuck his hands in his pockets. "Yeah, no thanks." He turned to Zaf. "Where's all the nightlife at? Where would you go?"

"The places I'd go wouldn't be your thing."

"Nowhere you can take me will be as dull as this." Ethan waved a hand at the low sofas and pot plants of the hotel reception. "No offence, Miss," he said to Penny.

"Me take you?" Zaf said. "No. I don't think—"

"Please?"

For a moment, Ethan's tough guy mask slipped. He looked like a kid who'd had a proper scare.

"I can't be held responsible for you."

"We're responsible for ourselves when we're out."

"Out?" Mrs Swinburne was crossing from the hotel entrance, nearly tripping over her bags as she did.

Ethan waved a hand. "Zaf's promised to show me a bit of the nightlife."

"Oh, has he?" said Mrs Swinburne. She sounded grateful.

Zaf sighed. He was going to regret this. "Right. Fine. I can come back in a while."

The group fidgeted into life, smiling at him.

"Wait a second, no!" Too late, Zaf realised what he'd got himself into. "Not everyone, I absolutely can't take you all out."

Ethan grinned and moved to stand beside him. "OK, I'll help you pick who to take. No suck-ups or losers, obviously. Sorry Ava."

"Like I would want to go anywhere you're going," Ava shot back.

"No, Ethan," said Zaf. "We are not picking favourites."

"Well man, it's up to you," replied Ethan. "Either we pick favourites or you take us all."

"This is very good of you," murmured Mrs Swinburne.

Zaf caught a flicker of sympathy on Penny's face. But he was caught in a trap he'd dug himself. And they had had a tough day...

"After dinner, I'll come back here and pick up anyone who wants to go out and see a bit of London nightlife. The dress code is disco fabulous, but don't worry if you don't have anything with sequins on it. If need be, you can sparkle from the inside."

The group buzzed with excitement. Zaf smiled back, but in his head, he could hear himself groaning.

## Chapter Eleven

To Diana, the Chartwell and Crouch bus depot was one of London's intrinsically magical places. Although it was hard to see the depot, with its peeling paint and grimed up windows, as a gem, those layers of paint and even the grime spoke of a long and fascinating history.

From the outside on Chiltern Street, the depot was just an anonymous frontage, but step through the 'catflap' of the human-sized door set within the bus-sized door and a visitor found themselves inside a vast space – wide, deep and with a great glass arch covering half the roof.

Newton Crombie had parked the bus among the other Chartwell and Crouch Routemasters, and laid out his sandwiches and thermos flask of tea on a little table by the bus before he started his clean-down routine onboard.

Diana turned to see Zaf enter through the catflap. He'd taken a while to extricate himself from the tour party.

"Everything alright?" she asked.

"Everything's fine." He gave her a brittle smile.

She couldn't blame him: they'd all had a challenging day.

"We should get our heads together and write up a report on what happened today," she said.

"What?" Zaf looked crestfallen. "Homework?"

"We either write it down and give it to everyone who's interested, or we can look forward to an excruciating set of debriefs with Paul Kensington."

"I don't give a monkey's what Paul's got to say," replied Zaf. "We've had a tough day and we deserve a medal for getting through it."

"Yes, you deserve a medal and yes, you do give a monkey's. Mr Kensington is our boss and he'll want to make sure the company isn't compromised."

"Fair point," huffed Zaf. "Give me twenty minutes."

"Twenty minutes?" Diana's eyebrows were raised. "Are you a speed typist?"

"I'll dictate it into my phone. We live in the future now, remember?"

"Also a fair point. I may or may not do something similar."

Zaf shrugged. "I'll be in the store room. Good spot to think."

Diana went into the kitchen and sat at the tiny table. It was an ancient thing that had gone out of fashion in around 1963, but the formica top was always clean, as was everything else in the mismatched kitchen. Chartwell and Crouch tours was a small outfit, and they had a set of ground rules for a harmonious workplace. The note taped to the inside of the cupboard door had evolved over the years, and Diana knew it by heart.

*Wipe the surfaces after eating, drinking and food prep.*

*Milk, tea, coffee, sugar and biscuits in the tartan tin are bought using the kitty and are shared. Other food belongs to someone and is not to be taken!*

*No double dipping with the sugar spoons!*
*Screwdrivers are NEVER to be used for stirring drinks.*

She settled into her chair and ran over the events in the Commons Chamber, playing everything back in her mind's eye as she dictated, being careful to include every detail. She also described the interactions with the police and the students after they'd been taken to the Robing Room.

She tapped her fingernails on the table as she finished, considering whether she might have missed anything. She didn't think so.

"Did you take my tuna sandwich?" asked Newton.

Diana looked up, startled by his sudden appearance. "No, I haven't seen it."

"I'm sure I put it on the table out there."

She shrugged.

"The plate's still there, but the sandwich has gone. I reckon someone's targeting me."

Newton Crombie was short, with grey-brown hair and a habit of wearing clothes designed to make him merge into the background. He was little more than half Diana's age, with a wife and whole gaggle of young children, but to Diana he had always had the air of someone older.

"Someone targeting you?" Diana said. "What makes you think that?"

"It happened twice last week. Tuna sandwiches both times. Targeted, you see."

"Or, maybe," she replied, "if you leave your tuna sandwiches out in plain sight then someone's going to assume they don't belong to anyone. Free sandwich."

Newton's eyelids twitched. "No such thing as a free sandwich, Diana. Never has been. Never will be."

"And maybe you could..." She waved her hand casually. "...

you could keep your tuna sandwiches in the fridge. Wrapped up. Like a, like a normal person."

Newton tutted. "Tuna needs airing. That smell is the histamines created in the cooking and canning process. It needs to breathe, to disperse. We don't want the histamines, do we?"

"Don't we?"

"Do you think if histamines were a good thing pharmacologists would have needed to invent anti-histamines?"

"That's something I've never found the need to ponder."

Diana stood up. *Time to back away.*

"I've installed temporary security cameras," he called after her. "They will reveal all."

"Right," she said. "I've got work to do."

"I thought you were just staring at your phone."

"Writing a report," she said. "We live in the future now, remember?"

She finished her report and emailed it to Zaf. She'd already received his, so she started to read it, looking for additional detail or conflicting memories.

As she was reading, she heard raised voices from out in the main body of the bus garage. She went out to find Zaf standing beside the bus and Newton lying underneath it, cleaning or maintaining some part of it. Zaf was yelling at Newton's feet.

"Why'd you think it was me? Like I'd steal your sandwiches. I've seen the bread you use, it's got birdseed in it!"

Newton wheeled himself out from under the bus. "Multigrain bread is better for you, everyone knows that."

Zaf turned to Diana. "I was listening to your dictation and he came in and started moaning about his stupid sandwich. I can't believe he'd accuse me like that, with no proof."

Diana sighed. "My fault, sorry. The conversation found its way into my transcript." She took a breath. "Let's just chalk it up to a stressful day, shall we? I'm sorry your sandwich went missing, Newton, but I don't know what we can do about it."

"If it happens again, I'll make sure I get evidence of who took it." Newton flung his polishing rag aside with a scowl.

"Mrs Bakewell!"

Paul Kensington, the company manager, was approaching from his little office with a look of deep annoyance. Diana sighed and prepared herself for a telling-off.

# Chapter Twelve

Paul Kensington always came to work in a short-sleeved shirt and tie. In an indefinable way that Diana had yet to unpick, his ties gave him the air of a schoolboy on his first day at big school, even though Paul – bald and with permanent rings under his eyes – looked like anything but a schoolboy.

He called Diana *Mrs Bakewell* even though he knew full well she was a Miss and that the only Mrs Bakewell was Diana's mum in her little flat in Bromley-by-Bow. He almost certainly did this to get a rise from her, something he seemed to do a lot. Like right now, collaring her just as she was about to leave for the day.

"What is it, Paul?" she said.

"Walk with me."

He turned on his heel and headed back to his office. "I've just got off the phone with a personal contact at the Redhouse Hotel."

"Personal contact? You mean Mike the caretaker."

"A personal contact," Paul repeated, "and I understand there was something of a hullabaloo during today's tour."

"We do aim to entertain."

"A dead body. Is that right, Diana? You're showing our service users dead bodies?"

"I prefer to call them tourists or, you know, just people," she replied. "And no, I didn't show them a dead body. We were in the House of Commons when, quite tragically, the young researcher showing us around was stabbed from behind."

Diana paused.

*From behind.*

She'd only said that because the knife had been sticking out of Florence's back. Which was interesting – if *interesting* wasn't inappropriate – because the obvious attacker, the protestor with the paint pot, had been in front of them all. The paint-throwing had drawn everyone's attention in that direction.

In fact, the protestor's actions had provided the perfect cover for whoever had wanted to attack Florence.

"Paul," she said, "I was just finishing up a report on today's events for you. Our tour group was caught up in the middle of the attack. You might have seen it on the news."

"You were there during the actual attack? Goodness. Sorry, I've been caught up in efficiency workshops all day at HQ. Lots to report though, some good outcomes at this location."

Diana felt her skin prickle. "Efficiency? Which areas are likely to be affected?"

Paul Kensington had taken a seat behind his desk. His office was small, dominated by a large and impressive desk and also, for reasons only he understood, a small Japanese zen garden in one corner. The square of pebbles and rocks was positioned so he could rake it from the comfort of his desk whenever he wished. He looked up at Diana.

"All areas will be affected by the efficiency proposals. Efficiencies in all areas. That's my personal expertise, as you know. Take your uniforms, for example, I bet you never give it a second thought, but we can save a lot there. I've run the numbers and my proposal went down a storm today, I can tell you!"

"I give my appearance quite a lot of thought."

Paul ignored her. "The new fleeces will be made in China, much cheaper. They'll be a baggy fit, so we don't need to stock so many sizes, and you can wear your own t-shirt underneath. Laundry bills will be slashed. Boom! And Paul Kensington's on course for his bonus!"

He clapped his hands in delight.

"Fleeces?" Diana asked.

"Branded fleeces. The company logo in nice bright colours."

Diana shuddered. "We get a lot of positive feedback on how neat our uniforms are."

"Pfft. Does neatness add money to the bottom line? Blazers are all very well, but the shirts and blouses are high maintenance. No, this is the way to go."

"And were there any more efficiency proposals?" Diana asked, dreading the answer.

"There were! The big one is my personal favourite. It'll save us an absolute fortune. I'll do a presentation to all staff, but here's a little heads-up. Have you ever heard of the Londiniumarium?"

"The what?"

"The Londiniumarium."

Diana tried to parse the ugly word in her mind and failed. "I can safely say I've never heard of it."

"It heralds the dawn of a new era in London tourism." Paul's gaze drifted upwards. "Why pay all the expensive parking fees and sit around in traffic jams to get to the locations when you can have everything under one roof in a single, immersive experience?"

Diana nodded for him to continue, although she was beginning to wish she'd never walked into his office.

"There's a warehouse space in Shoreditch where an entrepreneur has been building exactly that. Once visitors have checked in, they're led past an audio-visual display of the Thames. It even has smells pumped in so you can have a whiff of the river's faint sea-like tang. The film shows sights and sounds of the Thames. You get everything." He grinned. "Right up to watching Tower Bridge opening for a tall ship to pass underneath."

Diana leaned in, but Paul continued to garble away, unaware. "The next room has a video montage of London's greatest churches and cathedrals. There will be smells, candles for example. There'll be a government room of course, although most people don't want to dwell on politics, but they might want to sit in the Speaker's chair. There's a mock-up of that."

"You do know we're running a political tour this week, don't you? It's a school group, sponsored by their MP."

"Of course." He waved off her question. "The canteen will be outstanding. London-themed food with special napkins and such like. There'll be a bookable high tea option at a premium price, of course. Then they'll visit the palace room where pearly kings and queens will—"

"It sounds truly... inspiring." Diana just wanted him to stop talking. The whole thing sounded ridiculous. "But don't you think visitors want to experience things for themselves? People enjoy the personal touch, Paul."

"Do they? Do they really?"

"I get a lot of positive feedback."

His face screwed up. "My Aunt Ada owned a guest house in Southend. She thought it would be nice to put an old-fashioned china doll in each room. You know, the ones with the creepy eyes. And she would ask the guests, *what did you think of the dolly?* and they would say, *oh, the dolls are lovely*, because they wanted to be polite. And so my Aunt Ada, who quite possibly had a condition, put more dollies in the rooms, and when she asked more guests what they thought they, also being polite, would say... well, you get the idea. On and on it went, until there wasn't a chair or a shelf without a dolly on it. You see?"

Diana eyed him. "Am I meant to be the creepy dolly in this scenario?"

Paul pressed his lips tight. "We don't need creepy dollies on Chartwell and Crouch coach tours." He smiled at her. "Not that I'm saying you have a creepy face, Diana. You're like a daisy. Although have you had some corrective work done around...?" His pointing finger wandered in her direction. "Of course you haven't. Forget I said anything."

She gave him a plain, uncompromising look. Not quite one of Paddington Bear's famously hard stares, but at least a fraction of one.

"Your idea," she said. "The – what's it called? – Londiniumarium? It's..." She struggled to find the words. "It takes everything away from the real London. You could install one of these things anywhere you wanted to. You don't even need to be in London."

Paul Kensington straightened in his chair. "Diana, you're a

genius! That, of course, is the dream. A franchise operation with a Londiniumarium on every continent, in every major city. What a thing that would be! We are simply lucky enough to be the first tour operator to be offered the opportunity to explore the pilot facility. It's a real coup for us and it's in everybody's interest to make it work."

"Right."

"Just think how easy it will make your role! No more struggling to round up your group on a rainy street, no more having to do the same boring voiceover for each group. You'll be in a weatherproof environment and the headphones will deliver the commentary as each person makes their way around the exhibit."

Diana watched the excitement on his face. Was that for the concept, or for the money he believed he could harvest from it?

It would be the money.

Paul's understanding of people was on a par with Diana's understanding of the engine that ran the old Routemaster bus. She knew there was one in there, but if she opened up the bonnet, she wouldn't know where to begin. She wasn't even sure she'd be able to open the bonnet.

Diana stood. "Lovely chat, Paul. I hope I've put your mind at rest about the company's reputation being at risk after today's events. I need to get going now."

"Reputation?"

"The duty of care we have for our clients. I imagine people will have questions about how those young people became involved in today's situation. It'll all be fine once you've made your public statement though, won't it? Once you've popped it up on the website and emailed it around to the parents of the students, issued a press statement, that sort of thing. You've got everything you need in the report I emailed to you."

Diana walked out, feeling no sympathy about the work facing Paul Kensington before he could go home. He needed to take his head out of the clouds.

Beyond the doors of the Chartwell and Crouch bus depot, evening was settling over the capital. In a high-rise city, it was sometimes easy to forget that the sky was there at all, but this evening a gap between two buildings opposite gave a wide view of the setting sun and the tops of the houses in Mayfair. There were thin clouds in the sky, wispy strands of yellow beneath an orange evening sun. Diana's journey home to Ecclestone Square would be a pleasant walk.

She was about to set off when she remembered she didn't have her brolly. And then she remembered she'd left it on the floor of the chamber of the House of Commons.

Tutting at herself, she headed home.

# Chapter Thirteen

Diana walked to her home in Pimlico.

It was a couple of miles, but they were London miles and Diana was a firm believer that if a walk was interesting then it was no chore at all. It also gave her time to process the events of the day once more as she passed through familiar scenery.

From Marylebone to the shopping area around Oxford Street was busy, but Diana dodged shoppers with ease. She passed through Mayfair and on through Green Park and past Buckingham Palace, avoiding the crowds taking pictures of each other against the grand vistas of the palace building.

Diana knew how lucky she was to live in central London, and soaked up its glory at every opportunity.

Around Victoria Coach Station the tourists were more focused on their arrivals and departures, dragging large suitcases along the pavement with clickety-clack sounds.

London sometimes seemed entirely composed of tourists, a sea of faces – curious, naïve, cynical, apprehensive. The Palace of Westminster had been like that today. Interested and open faces, viewing the Houses of Parliament as nothing more than a historical theme park until that instant...

Diana turned past the St George's Tavern into Ecclestone Square. Huge white houses with columns and steps faced in towards the garden at its centre. It was a short distance to her front door, where she found a broad-shouldered police detective waiting with a coat over his arm and a duck-headed umbrella in his hand.

"Oh goodness, have you been here long?" she asked.

"Not particularly. I was enjoying a look around. You live in a very nice area. Very nice."

How did he make *very nice* sound like an accusation?

"I'm very lucky." Diana gave him a curious look. "I don't imagine detective chief inspectors normally drop off missing umbrellas in the early stages of a murder investigation."

He looked at the umbrella as if seeing it for the first time and, just for a moment, his square jaw broke into a smile.

"You seemed keen to get it back," he said. "Reginald, you say."

"He doesn't actually have a name," she said. "I may be a little past sixty but I'm not do-lally. You have a good memory for names."

"I remember everything. Today your group spent time in John Chapman-Moore's office. Is that correct?"

"The students went inside while Zaf and I waited in the corridor."

"You weren't in there with them?"

"The office was cramped. We had to wait outside."

"So inside the office, there was Chapman-Moore, his assistant Florence and the group of students?"

"He shares the office with another MP called Azar Mirza. It got so crowded that he had to leave too."

"I see." DCI Sugarbrook stared past her to the garden, his brow creased.

"Is the office relevant?" Diana asked.

"I can't share details of an ongoing investigation." Sugarbrook looked back at her. "But you drew our attention to the cup that you noticed in the Chamber, and there's a cup like it missing from Mr Chapman-Moore's office."

"And the murder weapon."

"What?"

"I was thinking about it," she said. "It's a knife, a brass knife. Nobody has a brass knife they use as an actual knife. And it's next to impossible to sneak any kind of weapon into the Palace of Westminster."

"Is that so?"

There was a challenge in Sugarbrook's voice.

Diana met his eye. "I imagine the weapon was a letter opener. It was already in the building, and you're so interested in his office…"

Sugarbrook nodded. "A letter opener that Mr Chapman-Moore has told us was a gift from a business partner when he sold his estate agency business in Leeds. It was engraved with his name."

So she was right.

"To answer your query then, Detective Chief Inspector, there was John Chapman-Moore and the twenty students from Foxwood Grange in the room with him. Azar was in there briefly. And Mr Chapman-Moore was chatting to someone outside his office just as we arrived."

"Who was that?"

"The Serjeant at Arms. Miss O'Grady."

"Hanna O'Grady. What were they talking about?"

Diana considered. "Rooms. Doors. Something like that. Perhaps he wanted a bigger office."

"Interesting."

"Is it?"

He looked at her. "All things are interesting in their own way."

Diana cocked her head. "So we know the protestor didn't carry out the murder."

"We? There is no *we*." Sugarbrook pointed at the gardens in the centre of the square, surrounded by iron railings. "A garden square is a peculiar thing, don't you think?"

"They are wonderful things," said Diana, "but not peculiar."

"I assume that you and the other residents have a key, but the public aren't allowed in, yes? It's not a park and it's not a garden. It's a peculiar relic of another time."

Diana pulled a face. "London is a city of relics. The trick is to honour the past while making our city workable for its current population. The garden squares form a corridor for wildlife. They're tended by people who know what they're doing."

"People who know what they're doing, couldn't have said it better myself." Sugarbrook smiled at her. "The police are grateful for your assistance, but we don't welcome people showing undue interest in our investigations. I hope that's clear."

Diana didn't like his frosty tone. "I wouldn't dream of getting in your way."

"As for Miss Arenosa—"

"Arenosa?"

He pulled a face at himself, irritated at letting the name slip. "The protestor. All eyes were on her in the chamber, so we can't rule out a connection. She'll remain in custody for the time being."

He raised a hand and walked off.

Diana wasn't sure she trusted the police not to take the path of least resistance. There was a corpse and there was a person in custody. It wasn't difficult to join the dots, no matter how improbable. They seemed convinced that Chapman-Moore was more important than poor Florence the victim.

Sometimes there was no justice. Diana didn't like that.

## Chapter Fourteen

"Good evening, Diana."

She turned halfway up the stairs. "Alexsei. How are you?"

Alexsei Dadashov was her neighbour, and the landlord of the building. He lived in the ground floor flat of the tall terraced house.

"Living the dream, Diana, you know this." He looked tired.

"You and me both, Alexsei. Is something wrong?"

"Of course not." He forced a smile. "My father has me looking after more of his places, and something always needs to be done, but it's fine. I am not a plumber, so I hire a plumber. I am not a painter, so I hire a painter. I do nothing but hire people to do jobs."

Alexsei had a complicated Russian-Azerbaijani heritage. His father managed his many properties, as well as his son, from afar.

"Can you learn how to do some of the things yourself?" she asked.

"It's not so easy!" he said, pushing back his thick hair. "I got a guy in to fit a new shower this week and I asked him to show me how it's done, to train me. Do you know what he said?"

Diana shook her head, trying not to laugh.

Alexsei swapped his mild Russian-Azeri accent for a broad and terrible faux-Cockney, and accompanied it with a swagger, thumbs tucked into his belt loops. "Yer jokin' ain't yer, treacle? If I shows yer how to do my job then 'ow on earth am I supposed to make a livin'?"

"He did not say *treacle*!" Diana was laughing hard now.

"He did. These people think I am some sort of little boy, just because I am so young and handsome." He straightened his back and tossed back his hair.

"You could find a plumbing course at a college, perhaps? It would do you good to get some practical skills."

"Perhaps. But my father would have opinions on this."

"He has opinions on many things," said Diana.

"Like the flat upstairs." Alexsei flicked his gaze up towards the ceiling. "My father is complaining that it is earning no money."

Diana's smile fell. "Bryan's place."

"I need to clear it out and get it on the market."

Bryan McGivern, her former neighbour and one of the few people she'd been able to call a real friend in the city, was dead. The whole house was quieter because of it. And more lonely.

Diana had spent many happy hours in Bryan's chaotic flat. Now it was reduced to a problem for Alexsei to solve.

"How will you clear it?" she asked. "He had no relatives."

Alexsei shrugged. "My father's solicitors sent someone. They said that the value of what's in there will pay for the clearance, so they will hand it over to a contract firm. Nothing moves quickly when a person dies."

"It's been six months." Six months and twelve days, to be

precise. "Let me go in and have a look around. I know those contract firms, they'll bundle up all Bryan's marvellous clothes for rag. I bet there are some lovely vintage pieces up there."

"He had shirts that looked like an accident in a paint factory."

"There were some bold patterns in the seventies and eighties," she said. "And you always admired his suits."

"Please, be my guest," said Alexsei, arms wide. "You knew Bryan, he would wish for you to take what you want."

"I'll take a look later in the week," Diana replied. "It's been a long day."

"Oh?"

Diana didn't have the energy to explain. "Oh, indeed," she said. "Good night, Alexsei."

## Chapter Fifteen

Bright and early on Tuesday morning, Diana left her flat and walked to work.

Setting out at roughly the same time every day meant that she saw a lot of the same people. It was heartwarming that central London, one of the busiest cities in the world, could feel like a village if you were willing to open yourself up to it.

She waved at two of her neighbours who were carrying mats to a morning yoga session in the garden square. There were several small lawn areas, perfect for communal events or group exercise.

A familiar face turned the corner. "Morning, Diana."

"Morning, Tobes."

They usually passed each other only briefly on the pavement, but it was good to know that Tobes was making his milk round. Diana believed strongly in having milk delivered. It would be cheaper to buy the large plastic cartons from the supermarket, but to her, the role of the milkman was worth a small premium. Whatever else happened, she could have milk and other essentials delivered to her door, and that was precious.

"Give me one of those pints if you would," she said. "They've switched to UHT sachets at the depot."

"Nothing wrong with UHT," said Tobes, passing over a cold glass bottle that she slipped into her handbag. "But nothing beats punching the foil lid of a pint of silver top, eh?"

She left the square and passed near to the coach station, with its soundtrack of wheeled suitcases. She was stopped twice for directions, and helped frazzled travellers find their way. Speaking to a pair of football fans struggling with a hangover, she threw in a suggestion for where they might find a decent breakfast.

Her morning walk took her on a different route past Buckingham Palace, this time along Grosvenor Place, where she stopped to get a coffee. The postman was emptying the letter box as she came out onto the street.

"Morning, Diana!"

"Morning, Asif! How did your son's interview go?"

"He made it through to the next round, we should know more next week."

"Best of luck to him. I know you'll miss him if he moves out, though."

"He must fly the nest. It makes perfect sense, although we will all be sad to see him go."

Diana walked on. She met dog walkers, taking their furry companions for their morning exercise. She often wondered where all of central London's dogs lived during the day. Garden space was at a premium, so their walks around the streets and in the parks were an important part of their lives.

She came to Park Lane. It was busy, so she continued walking on the Hyde Park side, where it was shady and pleasant under the trees. She glanced across at the Dorchester, where fancy cars sometimes indicated that celebrities were in attendance, particularly the ones that wanted to be noticed. Conspicuously parking a super-car in central London was the modern-day equivalent of the eighteenth-century Londoners who would dress up and bring their horses to Hyde Park, to be admired on Rotten Row, now a bridleway along the southern edge of the park.

Diana cut through towards Oxford Street, busy even at this early hour. At Selfridges she debated nipping into the food hall for a fancy yoghurt as a treat for later. But then she remembered Newton's meltdown over his tuna sandwiches. She wouldn't be surprised to find a trap of some sort inside the fridge: Newton sometimes allowed his engineering prowess to get in the way of his better judgement.

At last, she entered the cavernous gloom of the Chiltern Street depot. The main lights weren't on yet, so she flicked the switch.

"Morning." Newton stepped out of the kitchen space with a cup of tea.

Diana cocked her head. What was he doing, through there in the dark? "How are you doing, Newton?"

"Kettle's just boiled."

"And I've brought proper milk," Diana said, taking the pint out of her bag.

"The UHT's not that bad."

"That's what my milkman says."

"A wise chap." He grunted. "You remember when blue tits used to peck at the silver top lids of milk to get the cream underneath?"

She smiled. "You don't see that anymore, do you?"

"Little thieving beggars could ruin your morning cuppa

just to satisfy their own thirst. Here's an interesting fact for you."

"Oh, yes?"

Newton Crombie was a man full of interesting facts on all manner of subjects, not just his beloved buses.

"Blue tits learn how to do the milk trick, but they don't learn it from each other. They can't watch another bird do it and go *alright, I fancy a bit of that*. They don't have the right..." He tapped the side of his head. "Neurons! Don't have the right neurons. Each one of them has to discover it for themselves. You can't teach 'em, no matter how hard you try."

"That *is* an interesting fact," Diana said.

"Crafty creatures, though. A lot of clever thieves about." Newton tipped back his head of unruly hair and stared at the high ceiling and the beautiful glass arch. Diana could read his thoughts.

"Do you think blue tits stole your tuna sandwich?"

"No," he replied, eyes narrowed in suspicion. "But Ken Livingstone, when he was Mayor, used sparrowhawks to get rid of the pigeons in Trafalgar Square."

"So sparrowhawks stole your sandwich."

"Possibly not. I still don't know what happened. But on the other hand, I've got fresh sandwiches that I will take great care to protect. On balance, I would say that things are mostly fine."

Diana smiled. "Good. I think."

"Zaf's over there, by the way." Newton nodded at the area behind the bus. "Asleep. You should have words."

Diana approached the bus. There was a spare set of bus seats bolted to the wall. Whether it was a deliberately whimsical seating choice, or a convenient way to store spares in case the buses ever needed a replacement, she wasn't certain. Zaf lay across the seats, taking a nap.

She went back to the kitchen and grabbed some cups. She needed to wake Zaf, but a cup of tea would make the process more humane.

"Zaf, time to wake up." She gently shook his shoulder.

He murmured something unintelligible, but slept on.

"Zaf! You really do need to wake up," Diana said more loudly.

Nothing.

She gave his shoulder a sharp poke. "Zaf Williams, wake up!"

"Oh wow," he said, slipping into a seated position. "No need to shout. I was just having a little nap."

He said all of this with his eyes still closed. Somehow, he reached for the cup of tea that Diana offered and put it to his mouth all without opening his eyes.

"You sounded just like my mum then," he added.

"The woman's a saint, having to put up with you. You're all ready for work then, are you?"

"Mm-hm. Yep. Be ready whenever." He took another sip of tea and opened one eye slightly. He winced. "Bright, innit?"

"You're in a right state. What happened to you?"

"I will tell you, but please don't get mad or anything."

"Why would I get mad?"

"I took some of the students out."

"*The* students? *Our* students? Where were their teachers during – no, I don't know why I'm even asking. That pair are hopeless."

"The teachers said it would be OK. The kids wanted to see some nightlife, and I thought it'd be good to take their minds off things, y'know, after yesterday. I didn't let anyone under eighteen drink or anything. We did the Bluedog Club, the Marylebone Bar, down to the Fitzrovian."

Diana stared at him. "It's not me you need to worry about. It's Paul Kensington."

"Paul's alright."

"He is not, Zaf. He mustn't get wind of this. Who was it you took out? I bet it was that lad, er, Ethan. I can imagine he'd ask you."

"It was all of them."

"All of them? The entire group?" Diana tried to picture what that might even look like. "I don't know whether I should be angrier at you, or the teachers."

"Definitely the teachers. They're having an affair, y'know. All the kids say it."

"Don't believe what young people say to you, especially about their teachers." Diana sighed. "You got them back to the hotel safe and sound though, right?"

Zaf nodded.

"Come on, then. You need to get yourself together. Another day at the Houses of Parliament with Mr Chapman-Moore MP, hopefully less eventful than yesterday. Just a day of learning about politics."

"Ouch," said Zaf.

Diana wasn't certain if Zaf was complaining about his own ills or wincing in sympathy with the students.

## Chapter Sixteen

Newton pulled up outside the Redhouse Hotel, and Zaf and Diana stepped out to look for the students. They were milling around in reception, some of them slumped on the leather seats to one side. They looked worn out from the late-night partying.

Zaf's head was still pounding and his body felt like it was running on emergency power only.

*Teenagers*, he thought with some bitterness. Boundless energy and better than him at burning the candle at both ends.

One of the girls, Caitlin, waved a tired hand at him. Zaf managed to wave back.

Diana approached the teachers at the reception desk. "Mrs Swinburne, Mr Chaplin. Good to see you. I trust you'll be supervising your students *diligently* today."

"Yes, about that—" began Mr Chaplin.

"Sticking to them like glue, guiding them like shepherds around the halls of power, yes?"

"We were just discussing the itinerary," said Penny, behind reception.

"Oh?" said Diana.

"I took a call from the MP's office for the tour party. Mr Chapman-Moore. He's still helping the police with their enquiries."

"He's been arrested?" said Zaf.

"Gosh, I hope not. I just meant that he's busy with the police. And the House of Commons is still closed to the public. Won't be open again until Thursday."

"No Palace of Westminster, no tour guide," said Mrs Swinburne. "I suppose today's outing is cancelled. Possibly the next day's, too."

Zaf watched her, noticing the faint regret laced with relief at not having to do anything as dull as engage with her students.

"You've got a tour guide: me," said Diana. "And Zaf, of course. And there's more to British politics than the House of Commons. Come on everyone!"

She clapped her hands, setting off a series of small, painful explosions in Zaf's head. The students groaned.

"We'll have an excellent day of exploration and fun." Diana's voice was higher now, more painful. The students wandered outside, looking unconvinced.

Once they had all been counted onto the bus, Zaf turned to Diana. "Got a day of exploration and fun planned, have you?"

"Not yet," she murmured, "but give me a little time and I'll have everything in place." She stepped onto the bus to speak to Newton. "Take the scenic route, please Newton. I've got things to sort."

Newton nodded and put aside his phone, on which he'd been watching a grainy video.

"What's that?" asked Zaf.

Newton shoved the phone under his leg. "Secret reconnaissance project." He started up the engine.

Diana passed Zaf the wireless microphone. "They're all yours this morning."

"Really? My head—"

"I've got to sort out a day of fun and educational things. The guests are your responsibility and as for your head, well, that's your own fault."

Feeling he was being unfairly punished, but not having the energy to argue, Zaf took the microphone. He looked out of the windows.

"OK, people," he began, with an enthusiasm he didn't feel. "Anyone here familiar with Sherlock Holmes? Yeah? We're on Baker Street, his fictional home."

There was a minor flurry of interest as faces peered at the windows.

"Wow, what did he really look like?" piped up one of the lads. "Was he like Benedict Cumberbatch or the other one?"

"221B Baker Street was the *fictional* character's *fictional* home," said Zaf. "We know the TV series and the films in which he solves all those—" He stopped himself from saying *murders*, remembering the events of yesterday. "Crimes. He solved crimes. But it actually started out as a bunch of stories."

"Written by Dr Watson," said one of the girls.

"Again, *fictional*," Zaf said, "but over the years, people have wanted to visit the address from the stories. People go there because they want to surround themselves with all things Sherlock. Right, we're going to swing past Regents Park in a moment and then go right round and down to Marble Arch."

As Zaf spoke, he watched Diana, standing by the foot of the stairs and chatting on her phone. He had no idea who she was talking to but she always seemed to know who to get hold of in an emergency. Maybe by the time you got to her age, he thought, you just sort of got to know everyone.

By the time they'd passed Marble Arch and he'd given some general facts about the area (avoiding mention of the Tyburn gallows that had once stood nearby: another unnecessary reminder of death), Diana had finished her calls. She gave him a satisfied thumbs up.

The sightseeing seemed to distract the tired and hungover passengers. And throwing himself into his job had improved Zaf's own mood.

"Now, let me tell you about my favourite landmark," he said, his enthusiasm almost genuine now. "I reckon you'll like it too. Have a look over there at that big curved wall on the central reservation. This is Park Lane, by the way. It's pricey round here. Can you see that white curved wall? It's a monument to all the animals that have served in wars. As we go past, you'll see a horse and a dog. It's cute, isn't it? I can't pass this monument without giving it a little wave."

Zaf gave a wave to the animals on the monument and to his relief, so did most of the students. It was a small thing, but it was the beginning of the rapport that Diana liked to talk about.

"Brilliant view from here," he said, "although I always think the trees'll whack the bus as we go under."

The students on the top deck duly ducked, although they hadn't actually reached the trees yet.

Round the front of Buckingham Palace, they turned down Birdcage Walk. The traffic was light enough for them to glide down Great George Street and to their drop-off point outside the Palace of Westminster.

"Education awaits!" declared Diana.

Zaf stepped off the bus and, as he did so, a suited man in

glasses jogged up to meet him. It took a moment for Zaf to remember where he recognised him from.

"You're the MP, shares the office with the other MP," he said, knowing he sounded like an idiot.

"Azar Mirza." He grinned, and shook Zaf's hand. "Drafted in at the last minute to pour knowledge into young and eager brains."

Zaf recognised the words as something Chapman-Moore had said only the day before.

"Perhaps a little less of pouring things into brains, eh, mate?" suggested Zaf.

"Noted," said Azar, still smiling.

## Chapter Seventeen

As Diana stepped off the bus, she couldn't help noticing the increased police presence around the Palace of Westminster. The police were always around near the seat of British government, and it was almost unknown for half an hour to go by without the whoop of sirens. But today that watchful presence was more present than ever.

The murder of Florence Breecher had spooked people, although not necessarily for the right reasons.

Diana thanked Azar Mirza for stepping in to help them.

"The business of government keeps rumbling on," he said, addressing the whole group. "And that includes making sure your special visit goes ahead." He was not a tall man and had to stand on tiptoes to catch the eyes of the students at the back. "We can't go into the Palace of Westminster today, but that's not the only centre of British political life round here. Today, I want to take you to..." His hand swept round to the buildings across the road. "... Portcullis House."

When the students grasped which building he was gesturing at, they were visibly unimpressed.

"That's just an office block," said a girl.

"Bet that wasn't built by King William or nothin'," added Ethan.

"I'm impressed that you remembered about William Rufus," Diana said. "And, no, Portcullis House wasn't opened until two thousand and one, making it over nine hundred years younger than Westminster Hall. Is that right, Mr Mirza?"

"I wouldn't know about that," the MP replied with a shrug. "I'm more about what goes on in the buildings than the history of them. And it's Azar, please. Perhaps you can give us more details as we head over there?"

Diana raised her brolly to attract the group as they headed to the pedestrian crossing.

"Portcullis House was built because the Palace of Westminster doesn't have enough space for all the MPs' offices and administrative spaces. Nearly a third of MPs have their offices here. There's a tunnel right beneath our feet here, connecting those offices to the Houses of Parliament."

"A secret tunnel," said one young man.

"Perhaps, although it's not very secret."

"But it's still very Hogwarts, isn't it?"

"It does mean that members not lucky enough have an office in the Palace itself are never far from the action," said Azar.

"What's it like sharing an office with John Chapman-Moore?" asked Ava.

"I've learned a lot from watching such an experienced MP at work. And he has a lovely coffee-making machine."

Diana smiled: a politician's answer, if she'd ever heard one.

The lights changed and the group crossed.

"The site where Portcullis House stands has held many

buildings over the centuries," said Diana. "Before this, it was the home to the St Stephen's Club."

"A nightclub?" asked Ethan.

Diana grunted. "Not every club in London is a nightclub. The St Stephen's Club was a private members club for Conservative Party members, which moved out so that Portcullis House could be built."

Round the front of the building, where the Westminster Bridge crossed the majestic Thames, they came to the entrance and passed through the revolving glass doors to the security desks.

"The murderer might have snuck in this way," Ethan said to a friend.

Diana looked at him. "Let's just get on with our day and put that nasty incident from our minds."

"You kidding?" said Ethan. "A murder. We saw a flippin' murder, miss. Even when we were out at the clubs last night, it was all Ava could talk about."

Diana looked across at Ava. She seemed as tired as the rest of them but there was something else, too. As if the events were haunting her more than they were anyone else. Being that close to a woman as she lay dying... her hands around the knife blade, doing all she could to save Florence...

The interior of Portcullis House had none of the grandeur of the Palace of Westminster, but was a light and airy space. The central courtyard had a glass roof above and café seats where people could meet.

"Can we go sit down?" said a girl. "I'm shattered."

"It's only morning and you're all young and fit," said Diana. "We've got plenty to do today."

"This way." Azar beckoned them on. "We're going to the

largest meeting room, where a colleague of mine will give you a talk about the workings of government."

"Will there be chairs for us to sit on?" asked a boy.

"There will."

The students' mood shifted; Diana could sense relief.

She drifted over to Zaf as they followed Azar and the group.

"You did this," she said. "If there's any snoring during the talk it'll be your job to wake them up."

"I might be joining them." Zaf gave a pretend yawn which turned into a real one.

"Don't you flippin' well dare. And I'd like you to keep an eye on Ava."

"Ava? Why?"

"She was closest to what happened yesterday. I'm worried about her."

Zaf nodded, his expression grave. "Sure thing, Di."

She pulled a face. "It's Diana. Not Di, not Mrs Bakewell. Diana."

"Sure thing." He slipped through the moving group to be closer to Ava.

# Chapter Eighteen

Zaf sidled up to the gaggle of students around Ava and joined them as they walked into a meeting room with a large table at the front and rows of seats at the back. Like every group of humans ever put in this situation, the students avoided the front row, leaving the teachers alone there.

"I'll just go get my colleague," said Azar.

Zaf sat down with the girls and nodded at the screen at the front.

"Watch out, death by Powerpoint."

"Oh, don't," groaned a girl, Brianna. "Finchy, our history teacher, all of his lessons he just puts up a slide and reads it out. All of them, one by one."

Zaf shrugged. "School teaches you what the really boring jobs are like. Clock in, sit down in an office, clock out. The boredom's s'posed to inspire you to go do something less boring than your parents."

"My mum works in insurance," said one girl.

"Mine was an estate agent," said Ava.

"That's right, worked for whatisface," said Brianna. "My mum's a postie."

"Worthy professions, I'm sure," said Zaf. "Give me something where I'm meeting people all the time and being out and about."

"Like one of those people who stops you in the street and tries to sell you insurance."

"Maybe not that," replied Zaf.

There was movement at the front of the room. A slim woman in a suit had entered and was pointing a remote control at the screen.

"Hi, everyone. I'm Aneesha and I work for Mr Mirza. I gather you want to learn how Parliament works." The woman looked round expectantly. If she was hoping for a response, she didn't get it.

She clicked her remote to the first slide. "So, first question, what is democracy? Democracy comes from the Greek word *demos* meaning *the crowd* or *people*..."

\* \* \*

Fifteen minutes later, Zaf didn't know if he was awake or sleeping. He was floating in a horrible semi-conscious world composed of hard seats and a monotonous voice droning on about green papers and white papers and first and second readings. He suddenly snapped upright, sniffing sharply and blinking about him. Had he actually fallen asleep?

None of the students had noticed. Most had glazed eyes. A number had elbows on their knees and chins in their hands. But chirpy Aneesha hadn't noticed. On she went, her words a steady drone as she stood in front of a diagram showing a potential law being batted back and forth between the House of Commons and the House of Lords.

Zaf didn't actually need to be here. He was just the tour guide. If he slid outside, looking purposeful, no one would complain. He nodded thoughtfully, then silently excused himself and slipped off the end of the row to move towards the rear door. Diana's full attention was on Aneesha, and she didn't see him leave.

Across the corridor, Azar Mirza MP sat on the edge of a marble planter containing a huge fern or cheese plant or something. He stared at his phone, typing with two thumbs. He saw Zaf and put the phone to one side.

"You seem to spend all your time outside rooms," said Zaf.

"How's that?" asked Azar.

"Pushed out of your office by our tour group yesterday. Outside here today."

"It's the secret of being a politician," said Azar. "People think decisions are made in cabinet rooms or in the debating chamber but the truth is, they're not. Everything worth a damn in politics happens between one place and another."

"Is that so?"

"Ever watched *The West Wing*? All the important conversations happen in corridors."

"I'm more of a *Bridgerton* or *Game of Thrones* man."

"Live in the spaces between. That's the way to get things done." Azar looked at his phone and tapped. "And done."

Zaf fished for something to say. "Did you know Florence well?"

The MP blinked. "She was a powerhouse, an absolute dynamo. I don't know where she got the energy. In the office before anyone else. Still there when most of us had gone home and, if rumours were to be believed, partying all night every night."

"I'd like to know the secret to that."

Azar chuckled and gave Zaf a shrewd look. "You look done in, friend."

Zaf sighed. "I've just got out of a relationship. Malachi. It wasn't long term, not much more than a couple of months. It was never going anywhere, but it was fine while it lasted. And I was crashing at his place because – pff – London rent prices, right, and so I was sort of tied in with both boyfriend and accommodation. And now, now that we've split, I think I'm in free fall really. I'm like a boat that's had its rope cut. You know, um…"

"Adrift," said Azar.

"Right, man. Adrift. That's me."

"Or," said Azar, "you're just between one place and another. Waiting to get to that other place."

Zaf nodded, doubtful. "Florence. Did she have anyone? I mean, like, special. I know she shared a flat."

"That was a work colleague thing."

"I thought it was a cousin."

"Both, I think. They didn't seem close, though. I don't know if Florence had anyone special apart from…" Azar drifted off and swallowed hard.

"Apart from?" said Zaf.

"I'm not a gossip."

"Whereas I absolutely am. Do tell." Zaf saw the hesitation in the MP's face. "She's beyond being hurt, and I'm sure you'll only speak well of her."

Azar smiled. "You are either naively optimistic or you're trying to manipulate me." He glanced about. "There were always rumours."

"Rumours?"

"Of an affair with John Chapman-Moore."

"The..."

Zaf wasn't naïve, whatever Azar thought. But John Chapman-Moore was at least twice Florence's age. More. Zaf tried not to judge people on appearances, but the contrast between the lively young woman and the flabby older man was too stark to believe.

"I suppose," he began, "she was pretty and he was rich, right?"

Azar tilted his head. "She had ambition and he has power." He shook his head. "Rumour isn't the right word. John's behaviour towards young pretty women is an open secret. Apparently, he's been like it since before coming here." He twisted his lips together. "It's not a case of *if* he was having an affair but one of *when* and *who with*."

# Chapter Nineteen

"Any questions?" Aneesha looked round the group, her face glowing.

Diana peered about at the students. They looked stunned, dazed or quite possibly anaesthetised. Even the teachers didn't seem to realise the lecture was over. Mr Chaplin was focused on picking out pieces of lint from the zipper of his coat.

"Well, that was fascinating," Diana said. Yes, it had been a little dry in places. But Aneesha had done her best to present the information clearly and with as little jargon as possible.

"Perhaps I should go on to explain how sub-committees work," said Aneesha.

Diana could see that this group wouldn't appreciate that level of detail.

"I think it's time for some fresh air and time to reflect," she said. "A walk round Parliament Square, anyone?"

A few groggy heads turned her way.

"Outside," she said. "Fresh air. Maybe a chance to grab a drink."

Some of the students pulled themselves to their feet.

"Good. This way, then," said Diana. "Mr Chaplin! Mrs Swinburne! You might want to lead your students outside."

Grumbling as much as any of the teenagers, the two teachers shuffled to the front of the group and led the way.

Outside, the fresh air brought some life back to the group. As they waited among other tourists to cross back over the road to Westminster Palace, the girl Ava Franks slipped in beside Diana.

"Aren't we going to see Mr Chapman-Moore today?"

"Not today," Diana told her. "What with everything that happened yesterday, he's needed elsewhere."

"But we are seeing him again?"

"Probably. But just because this trip is organised by him, doesn't mean we have to shadow him everywhere. You seem very keen."

Ava pulled a face. "He's our MP. He's meant to serve our constituency."

"And do you think he's doing a good job?" Diana asked.

"Everyone needs to be held to account."

The lights changed and they all crossed. Ava slipped away to rejoin her friends.

"She got a thing for Chapman-Moore?" Zaf whispered, drawing close to Diana. "You do know that John Chapman-Moore was having an affair with Florence Breecher?"

"You've got affairs on the brain today," Diana said.

"Well, that MP, Azai. He says Chapman-Moore was a well-known philanthropist."

"You mean philanderer."

"Do I?"

"Was he having an affair, or was he giving lots of money to charity?"

"The first one."

"Philanderer."

"Although he was behind that big bill to find homes for the homeless. That's..."

"Philanthropic. Nice save, Zaf."

Zaf and Diana were ahead of the pack of students.

"D'you think Ava might have had anything to do with it?" said Zaf. "The murder, I mean."

Diana looked back at the students. Ava was talking animatedly to Azar. The MP was grinning, apparently delighted to engage with some of the electorate, even if they weren't his constituents. Or, for the most part, old enough to vote.

"Ava, linked to the murder?" said Diana.

"Obsessed with her MP. Maybe fancied him herself. I mean, I don't see the appeal myself. Dude's a chubby old guy, like Santa without the hair or the charisma, but then, I'm not a straight girl, so..."

"Did I mention that Chief Inspector Sugarbrook was waiting for me at home last night?" Diana said.

"He thinks *you* did it?" said Zaf, shocked.

"I should hope not. The murder weapon was a brass letter-opener taken from John Chapman-Moore's office."

"Oh. So no one smuggled it in."

"It was already in the Palace. And specifically in Chapman-Moore's office. So the police are wondering who had access to the office. John himself, but stabbing your own researcher with your own letter-opener is perhaps too stupid, even for an MP. Azar back there. Any researchers who work there."

"And our tour party," said Zaf. "They were all crammed in there."

"Any one of them could have taken it if it was openly on display."

Zaf made a deep and troubled humming sound.

"Hmmm?" said Diana.

"It might be nothing..."

"Most things are."

"When they all came out of the MPs' office," Zaf said, "before we went to the Commons Chamber, I saw Ava with her hand under her jacket. Like this..." He put one hand against his stomach and wrapped over it with his other hand and his open jacket. "Like she'd hurt her hand and she was using her jacket as a sling or covering. And when I saw her face..."

"What?"

"I thought she was in pain. Maybe unhappy and confused. But definitely guilty when she saw me looking."

"You think she stole the letter-opener?"

Zaf shrugged.

"Let's not forget the cup," said Diana.

"The cup found next to the body?"

Diana nodded. "The oddest thing, I thought. It had no right to be there in the Commons. What if that was what Ava was carrying under her jacket?"

"That doesn't make much more sense," said Zaf. "Who steals a cup and carries it away under their school jacket? A cup thief?"

"Maybe just a politics groupie? And you suggested she might have a *thing* for Chapman-Moore."

"He's old enough to be her dad. Maybe her granddad."

Diana shrugged. Zaf was mature enough to know that hardly mattered.

"Besides," said Zaf, "the murderer didn't have to steal the

knife that morning, at that moment. Anyone who had access to the room could have taken it. Security staff, cleaners, whatever."

"True, but DCI Sugarbrook was interested in the fact that the Serjeant at Arms was arguing with Chapman-Moore outside his office."

"The woman in the oldie-timey clothes?"

"You are a trained tour guide, aren't you, Zaf?" she said.

"Oh, there are so many people with silly outfits, silly sticks and silly titles in that place. Master doorkeeper and senior seat waxer and—"

"You're making it up. The Serjeant at Arms. Hanna O'Grady. And the walking stick isn't part of the uniform. She has real power. If the Palace of Westminster was a frontier town, she'd be the sheriff. If someone's up to crooked business then she's the one who works with the police to sort it out."

Zaf grinned. "Crooked business. These are politicians we're talking about."

Diana smiled. "Has tiredness made you cynical, Zaf?"

"I *am* tired."

"Your own fault, disco boy. But maybe Chapman-Moore was up to something dodgy."

"And Florence was killed for getting too close to the truth."

"Idle speculation?" Diana pursed her lips. "I know Hanna. Sort of. She's one of the alto baronesses."

"Alto baronesses?"

Diana shook her head, dismissing his question. "I know *of* her. I could get to speak to her if I wanted."

Zaf gave her a look. "We're not the cops, remember?"

"I know. I... I don't know if they're taking Florence's death seriously enough. They're making it all about Chapman-Moore. Maybe we are, too."

Up ahead in Parliament Square, the anti-poverty protestors were being as colourful and as noisy as the day before.

"The police have a woman in custody," Diana said as they approached the protestors. "The one with the paint. Miss Arenosa, DCI Sugarbrook called her."

"You think they'll pin it on her?"

"I don't know. I've not yet decided what kind of man Sugarbrook is."

## Chapter Twenty

They stepped across into Parliament Square. The square was wide and the field of green grass at its centre was attractive, if only for bringing a note of colour to the grey-white heart of the city.

Diana raised her umbrella to draw the attention of her tour party.

"I hope a bit of exercise has woken you up again. It's nearly lunchtime but before we sort you out with food, I'm hoping your teachers will take you on a short tour of the statues around Parliament Square."

"We will?" said Mrs Swinburne.

Diana gave her a steely gaze.

"I'm sure you'll do a great job," she said. "If you're looking for a place to start, you might recognise Winston Churchill over there."

"Remember, kids," said Zaf, "see how many women and brown people you can spot. I'll be expecting names later."

Muttering between themselves, Swinburne and Chaplin led the students in a procession around the square.

"You could do this bit of the tour," Zaf said. "You love talking up a statue."

"I might step in at Abraham Lincoln or Millicent Fawcett." Diana pointed. "But I fancied having a little chat with *them*."

Zaf followed her finger. "The protestors?"

She nodded. "Coming?"

"Of course," he replied, with a dramatic waggle of his eyebrows. "I can ask them about their placard. Is it *No More Fat Cats* or *No Fat More Cats*?"

Diana rolled her eyes, but she was pleased Zaf was back to making jokes. Had he even been to bed last night? He'd not been right since Monday morning: splitting up with Malachi seemed to have hit him harder than he wanted to admit.

Diana moved through the crowd. There were people with placards, others sitting on the ground, where a collection bucket was labelled with a large arrow asking for donations. A woman moved amongst the crowd, distributing drinks to the other protestors.

Diana approached her. "Hi. Were you here yesterday?"

"I was." The woman's reply was terse, her accent faintly European. "Are you a journalist?"

"Nothing like that. I'm Diana."

"Giselle," replied the woman, still wary.

"I was in the Chamber with a tour group yesterday."

"Chamber?"

"The House of Commons, when your colleague threw the paint."

"Are you about to give us a dry-cleaning bill?"

"Nothing like that," said Diana.

The woman looked Diana up and down. "I hope it didn't go on you. But you have to make a statement if you want to make an impact."

"I didn't get covered in paint," Diana replied. "Only blood."

Giselle's face darkened. "That was a bad business. It's why they still have Catalina locked up. They say it's for questioning, but I don't know what they can be asking her. There have always been political prisoners."

"I don't think she was exactly a threat to the government."

The woman grunted. "They seem convinced she was involved, so they're hanging on while they try to pin it on our group."

"So you don't think she was involved in the attack on the researcher then?"

Giselle pursed her lips, giving Diana a steely glare. After a moment, she said, "Catalina made us get vegan paint for the stunt in the chamber. Vegan. Paint."

"I didn't know there was such a thing," said Diana.

"I'm surprised there's *non*-vegan paint, said Zaf.

"Totally organic and free of solvents," said Catalina. "She went to Bethnal Green to buy it from this little art shop. I reckon you could pour it on your cereal and eat it, although it'd make for an expensive breakfast." She looked Diana in the eye. "Catalina wouldn't be a part of hurting someone. She'll be hurting right now, knowing someone lost their life in that incident. By the time the police have finished with her she'll be convinced it's her fault."

"It is a coincidence that someone would choose that exact moment to stab someone," Diana pointed out.

"Is it?"

"It has occurred to me that the House of Commons is a terrible place to attempt a murder. There are cameras everywhere. I'm assuming it's only because of the chaos Catalina caused that there isn't footage of the person who stabbed Florence."

Giselle nodded slowly. "Florence."

"She was a nice young woman, from the little I knew of her."

"A willing servant of the capitalist elite." Giselle's cheek twitched. "But no one deserves death, do they?"

"Not in my experience," said Diana.

"But nothing surprises me." Giselle wagged a finger at the Palace of Westminster. "That place is filled with opportunists. They see something and immediately they're thinking *how can this benefit me?* Even when they're being 'good' there's always an angle."

Diana followed her gaze. "Means, motive and opportunity."

"Exactly. Catalina just gave them an opportunity. If the police would just figure out the means and the motive then maybe they'd find out who really did this."

There was the clink of coins as someone threw change into the collection bucket.

Diana looked over. "Fighting poverty by collecting coins. Doesn't it feel like a drop in the ocean?"

"It's not just about the money," said the woman. "Every time someone drops a coin in there it's a show of support. It's a validation of our work."

"Fair enough." Diana fished in her pocket for some change.

## Chapter Twenty-One

Diana might have thought he was joking, but Zaf really did want to ask the protestors about their placards. Diana left him to it, wandering across Parliament Square towards the school party from Foxwood Grange.

The words *means, motive and opportunity* circled in her head. It was always possible that the target of the attack had been John Chapman-Moore. But either way, the person who had killed Florence had the means and the opportunity and, depending upon their true target, the motive as well.

The means was the brass letter-opener. That was available to anyone who'd been in John Chapman-Moore's office, either on the day itself or at some point in the past. As Zaf had suggested, a worker in the Palace could have picked it up, assuming Chapman-Moore wouldn't have noticed its absence. As for opportunity, that did seem to circle round Catalina Arenosa's paint-based protest. Either the killer had seen Catalina's demonstration and leapt into action on the spur of the moment, or he or she had been willing to take the risk of being spotted. Which would make the two things purely coincidental, a convenient, unlooked-for distraction.

Diana hummed to herself. Life was full of things that seemed to just come out of the blue but, in her experience, it didn't do to try to explain them as mere coincidences.

Nonetheless, someone had to have the means, access to the office, and opportunity, to be there in the Commons, in order to have killed Florence. That included the students and John Chapman-Moore himself.

Azar Mirza? The Serjeant at Arms Hanna O'Grady? Neither of them had been in the Commons Chamber at the time...

"No," Diana murmured, suddenly remembering.

After the attack, when security came swarming in, Hanna had been there. Diana had seen her, stepping in from behind the Speaker's chair, as though appearing from the wings of a theatre stage.

"She was there," Diana said to herself.

The students were halfway round the square now, past Lloyd George and Palmerston. They were heading for the Gandhi statue, the teachers no doubt confident that they had more to say about the Indian independence campaigner than about prime ministers from over a century ago.

Azar Mirza was loitering at the rear of the party, showing polite interest.

"We're not keeping you from anything, are we?" said Diana as she stepped in beside him.

The man wrinkled his nose in amusement, making his glasses shift. "Would you believe me if I said I went into politics in order to do this stuff?"

"Follow bored teens round London?"

"Engage people in politics, encourage them to participate."

"Hmm." Diana considered. "I don't know if I believe you."

"Would it help if I told you I'm from an insanely wealthy family and I've never had to do a day's work in my life, and this politics thing is very much a hobby?"

"That suddenly sounds plausible."

"I'm not saying it's true, but I'm glad you find it plausible."

"Can I ask you a question?" she said.

"Always."

"Was John Chapman-Moore up to something dodgy?"

Azar gave a loud and involuntary blast of laughter, and immediately made apologetic faces to people standing nearby.

"I'm sorry, Diana, did you just ask me if John Chapman-Moore MP is corrupt?"

"It was just a question. I didn't mean to offend…"

Azar spread his hands, as though warming up for an explanation. "The man is wealthy, not wealthy like my business magnate dad is wealthy but definitely wealthy. His money is in real estate. He owned a number of property businesses up north before his political career brought him south. Sold them off and moved into the London property market. It's no accident that he's got himself onto certain sub-committees and fought for certain bills."

"I thought his latest project was that *Helping the Homeless* thing," she said.

"*Helping Hand for the Homeless*," he said. "Sure, but even that's about getting tenants into houses. Property, ownership, rents. John Chapman-Moore lost the Tory whip and, to be honest, to keep the Tory whip you just need to turn up and vote and make sure you don't wind up on the front pages of the sleaziest tabloid papers. The man has no moral compass. He sold it."

"So, he's corrupt."

"I didn't say that," said Azar. "I said he was a politician."

"You don't like him."

Another chuckle. "If I may quote Mark Twain. *I admire him, I frankly confess it; and when his time comes I shall buy a piece of the rope for a keepsake.* John Chapman-Moore swims in the world of politics, whereas I only paddle in its shallows."

Azar was wrong about himself, Diana thought. He was as much a politician as Chapman-Moore. He'd managed to say a dozen things without saying anything at all.

"Can I be blunt, then?" she asked. "Was Hanna O'Grady investigating him for corruption?"

Azar sucked in his cheeks as he thought.

"The Serjeant at Arms is not a police officer," he said, eventually. "She has power and influence, but her role is not to weed out the evil in the heart of government and expose it to the light of judgement."

"No?"

"Absolutely not. Her role is to protect Parliament, to serve it, to maintain its integrity and to make sure we have a functioning democracy. Sometimes the Serjeant at Arms might weed out corruption in Parliament. Sometimes..." He gave her a playful look. "Sometimes, the right thing to do is to bury it so deep, no one can ever find it."

Diana drew back, surprised at his cynicism. He seemed unfazed.

"If John was involved in something," he said, "and I'm not saying he was, then I'd put a hundred pounds on Hanna knowing everything about it. She's no fool."

"No, she is not."

"You know her?"

"She's an alto baroness. I'm an occasional stiffener."

He frowned. "Am I supposed to know what those words mean?"

Diana was about to explain when she caught some words coming from Mrs Swinburne's mouth.

"Suffragist, not suffragette, Mrs Swinburne," Diana corrected, stepping forward to the statue of Millicent Fawcett, the Edwardian campaigner. "Boys and girls," she continued, swinging her duck head umbrella, "who can tell me the difference between a suffragette and a suffragist?"

Two dozen faces looked at her blankly.

"Very well." Diana smiled. "Then it's time for a history lesson!"

## Chapter Twenty-Two

All told, Diana decided, it had not been a terrible day out. A lecture on the workings of government and a gentle stroll around Parliament Square followed by a wander along the Embankment, where the breeze off the Thames revitalised flagging spirits. And then the bus ride back to the hotel. Just about sufficient for a day out.

Diana and Zaf went into the Redhouse Hotel with the students while Newton returned the bus to the depot. Penny on reception was already guiding the group through to the dining area.

"And what treats have you got lined up for tomorrow?" Penny asked Diana.

"That's a closely guarded secret," she replied, in lieu of telling the woman she had no idea.

"Any particular history we need to brush up on?" said Mr Chaplin, who'd been unable to identify more than four of the twelve statues in Parliament Square.

"No." Diana allowed herself a smile. "Although you might

want to read up on the Supreme Court, Oliver Cromwell's Commonwealth and the Restoration."

"Er, right."

Zaf and Diana stepped out onto Chiltern Street.

"D'you think you can avoid being dragged into more ill-advised nights on the town with the students?" Diana asked.

"Don't! It might just kill me. I hope they're having a restful evening in the hotel."

They stepped through the door-within-a-door into the depot. Newton was conducting a walk-round check on the bus.

"You were chatting to those protestors for a while," Diana said to Zaf.

"You're always talking about the importance of networks. I asked about the placard and whether they'd be open to a re-design." Zaf shrugged. "I could knock up a couple of prototypes for them. It would be nice to keep my hand in, artistically speaking."

Diana nodded. His networks would be different from hers, wouldn't they?

"What did you have in mind, art-boy?" asked Newton, breaking out his polishing rag to wipe down the headlights.

Zaf turned to him, his eyes bright for the first time that day. "First of all, there's the super-simple version." He raised a hand, air-writing the words as he spoke. "*Fat Cats Out!* Just those three words make it much more effective. Boom! Boom! Boom!"

"Yep, I see that. What else?"

"A cartoon picture of a fat cat, obviously."

Newton turned to Zaf with a look of concern. "You can't do that. Too cute. The point about fat cats is that people don't like them. They can't be cute."

"Good point." Zaf cocked his head. "I could make it look superior and a bit angry?"

Newton rolled his eyes. "Cats look like that anyway."

"I could give it a top hat and one of those pairs of glasses where there's only one."

"A monocle," Diana suggested.

Newton looked unsure. "Still sounds a bit too cute. Why not have it eating buildings and people? Make it like a terrifying Godzilla cat on a rampage through the city." He took his phone out of his pocket. "Anyway, I need to check my footage."

"Footage?" said Zaf.

"A camera and a sacrificial tuna sandwich," he said. "The thief may soon be revealed." Newton beckoned them to follow him to the kitchen.

As Diana turned, she saw a figure by the door of the depot. It was framed by light from the sunny street and all she could make out was the silhouette of a young woman with long ginger hair. For a split second, she thought it was Florence Breecher.

*No,* she told herself. *She's dead.*

Diana stepped forward, the angle of the light changed, and she realised it wasn't Florence but her cousin.

"Tabitha?"

"I'm sorry," said Tabitha. "I didn't know where else to go."

Diana hurried to her. "Is everything OK?"

There was a pained look on the young woman's face. "You spoke so kindly of Florence. And the police... I don't think they're interested and..." She held up a document folder she'd been gripping in both hands. "Someone needs to see this."

Diana ignored the folder for now. The priority here was the upset young woman.

"Would you like a drink?" she asked, glancing about. "Not

here. I know a nice place just down the road. Paninis, pastries." She smiled. "My treat."

"That's very kind." The tension in Tabitha's body relaxed.

*Tasty For You*, despite its clunky name, was one of Diana's favourite little cafés. The place was clean, the tablecloths eclectic and the owner, Levon, always friendly.

She directed Tabitha to a table in the window and ordered tea for two and a mozzarella melt for the young woman. Tabitha pushed the folder towards Diana, her gesture secretive. Diana thought of Cold War spies passing documents to each other on Hyde Park benches.

"It's Florence's," Tabitha said.

The folder was a wrap-around wallet, stiff with a velvety exterior like an expensive notebook. Diana opened it.

Inside were piles of papers and a slim diary. As she lifted it, a wooden biro fell out and landed on the floor. Tabitha bent to pick it up and put it on the table.

"One of her work folders," Tabitha said. "I was tidying through her things. Sorting things out."

The folder carried the faint leather-and-brass smell of Parliament, bringing a smile to Diana's lips.

"You were sorting through her things?" she asked. "So soon?"

Tabitha shook her head, her gaze on the table. "The place is so quiet without her. I've got nothing to do but revise for my resits but without Florence... it's hard to focus."

"What are you studying?"

"Political Science at LSE. I struggled this year."

"It's a prestigious university," said Diana. "And you're working in Parliament as well."

"Oh, just menial work for the facilities team. A bit of money and a chance to be at the heart of the action."

Diana flipped through the folder's contents. Most of the papers were computer print-outs. There was a small number of hand-written pages. She spread them out: maps and details of properties.

"What is this? And why bring it to me?" she asked.

"Florence worked for this MP, Chapman-Moore. She was very interested in him."

"She was?" Diana remembered Zaf's comments about an affair.

"His business dealings. He owns a lot of property."

"So I gather."

"This isn't work stuff." Tabitha tapped the edge of the folder. "This is private research."

Levon came over with the mozzarella melt. Tabitha didn't speak again until he was back behind his counter. "She was snooping into his business deals. She thought he was up to something."

"Something?"

"Something criminal. Why else would she be keeping a folder on him at home?"

"I thought this was a work folder," said Diana.

"Work, home. She was keeping it away from him." Tabitha tugged at the diary in the folder and flipped it open. The pages were full of scrawled appointments and notes. Lots of abbreviations. "I don't understand all of this, but..."

Diana frowned at one of the notes. "Tiger Tiger?"

"That's a nightclub. She was a party animal."

"And Village Underground," said Diana. "That's one too."

Tabitha nodded. "Last week, the week before..."

Diana looked into her eyes. "Before. Yes. I know."

A sniff. "That week, she was being super secretive. Coming back late at night."

"Partying?"

"Yes. She was never quiet coming in. I'm a light sleeper."

"Not a party animal yourself."

"I love a good party, but if I don't pass these resits then I'll have to re-do the year. And uni is so expensive. But I think this…" She put a finger on the folder. "It was coming to a head somehow."

Diana looked at the week in the diary. There were work meetings and initials. JCM – John Chapman-Moore – came up a lot. And there were social appointments too. The night before Florence's death, she'd clearly been to a place called the Hog Club on Berkeley Street. Below today's date there were the words *Tab's Party*.

"Your birthday."

Tabitha smiled weakly. "She wanted to throw me a party to cheer me up. Always… she always wanted to help people."

Diana sat back and took a deep breath. "Eat your melt while it's still melty."

Tabitha obediently took a bite. Diana sipped her tea and thought.

"You think Florence was investigating some sort of corrupt behaviour John Chapman-Moore was involved in."

"I do."

"And you suspect her death is somehow linked to that."

Tabitha made a helpless gesture, her mouth full of toasted panini. "I think it is."

## Chapter Twenty-Three

Diana's fingers rested on the folder of information Tabitha Welkin had presented to her.

"And so this is evidence?"

"Could be," Tabitha said.

"I should take it straight to the police."

"I don't mind," Tabitha replied. "Whatever you do, I know it'll be the right thing."

"So quick to trust me."

"You cared. I could tell."

Diana nodded. "You don't trust the police."

"I don't want to be seen to be interfering."

Diana laughed.

"What?" said Tabitha.

"You think the police are more used to old ladies like me interfering."

Tabitha hesitated. "You seem to get more respect the older you get."

"Trust me, it doesn't look like that from the other side of the age gap."

"Still." Tabitha put her hands together, as if cleansing them of her connection to the folder. Her fingers were pink and shiny: the weathered fingers of a worker, not a student.

Diana picked up the dropped pen. It had the maker's name, *Bambubu*, and a little leaf logo on the side. She scrawled her mobile number on a napkin.

"Get in touch if you need to," she said. "And make sure you work hard on your revision."

"I intend to."

Diana stood up. "Enjoy the rest of your sandwich."

"You're going?"

"There's someone I need to speak to. They'll be very interested in this." She tucked the folder under her arm and looked towards Levon. "A refill and a slice of cake and anything else she wants," she told him.

"Sure thing, Diana," he replied.

As she left the café, Diana took out her phone and found the number for Simon Smallchild, the parliamentary estates manager she'd bumped into in the Central Lobby the day before.

He picked up almost instantly.

"Diana!" he boomed.

"Simon! I know it's late—"

"I'm on my way to rehearsals now."

"Right. I wondered if you still needed a stiffener."

"Oh," he said. "I'm sure the director would be delighted, but I'd have to check with the altos."

"Please do. You know how I love Rachmaninoff."

"Let me ask." He hung up just as she stepped back into the Chartwell and Crouch depot.

Newton stuck his head out of the kitchen area. "Come here and look at this."

"Your camera footage?" Diana asked.

Zaf peered round the doorway at her. "The man's got these tiny spy cameras."

Newton had placed his phone on a little stand on the table. "Behold! I have captured footage of the tuna thief."

"Was it Paul Kensington?" Diana asked.

Newton ignored her, pointing at the screen. It showed Newton's sandwich, sitting on a plate on the kitchen table.

Newton indicated the timestamp. "Twenty minutes after we left, look who comes along."

A tabby cat crept into view on the screen. It looked around as it approached, seeming at one point to stare directly into the camera. It was neither a fat moggy nor a scrawny stray but a proud and sleek creature, full of a proud confidence that made Diana assume he was a tom.

Satisfied it was safe, the cat moved into the centre of the screen. It licked the side of the sandwich, tasting the tuna. After a moment, it grabbed a corner of the sandwich in its mouth and dragged it backwards out of shot.

Newton paused the video. "See! See!"

"I do," said Diana.

"So where is it?" Zaf looked around, as if expecting to find the cat there in the room with them.

"Good question," said Newton. "The next part of my investigation will reveal all. I very much want to meet our mystery visitor."

"I wonder if we could get it to wear a top hat so I could sketch it for a placard?" Zaf said.

Newton and Diana both gave him a look.

"What? I mean, didn't you see the way it turned to look at the camera? Classic wicked cat."

Diana smiled. Zaf nodded at the folder. "What was that woman doing here?"

"Grieving in her own way, I think," said Diana. "I need to deliver this to someone who can make sense of it."

"Oh?"

"In my role as a stiffener, I hope to bump into Hanna O'Grady."

"A stiffener?" Zaf gave her a sly look. "I had no idea you were into things like that."

Newton looked both fascinated and appalled.

"You don't know what a stiffener is, either of you?" Diana asked.

"Um, no," said Zaf.

"I mean I might...." Newton bluffed.

"It simply means that I'm offering my guest services to a choir."

"Oh?" said Zaf. "Oh." His tone was disappointed.

"Stiffeners stiffen singing?" asked Newton.

"Outside support. Like ringers on a sports team." Diana looked at her colleagues. Sports analogies were wasted on them.

"Stiffener, huh," grunted Zaf. "They need to find another name for that. Seriously, they do."

"A friend is inviting me as a favour," Diana told him.

Diana was comfortable with the currency of favours. Her approach was to build up a stock of goodwill with all of her casual acquaintances, and then once in a while, when she needed a favour, to ask for it directly. She was rarely refused, so she reckoned her method was a good one.

"So, if you're a stiffener, a ringer, that must mean you're a good singer," Zaf observed.

Diana cleared her throat. "I've had the privilege of singing in all sorts of places."

Zaf raised his eyebrows. "Is this where you tell me that you've done backing vocals on a hit single?"

Diana winked at him. "Uncredited, but yes. More than one."

"That might be the coolest thing I ever heard in my life."

"Later." Diana smiled. "Or I *will* be late."

Holding the folder and grabbing her brolly, she made for the door. If she hurried, she could get there before the rehearsals began.

# Chapter Twenty-Four

Diana met Simon Smallchild beyond the security checks at Parliament's Cromwell Green entrance. He greeted her with a warm hug, his wiry mutton-chop whiskers squashed against her cheeks.

"It's been too long!" he said.

"It has," she agreed. "I'm glad you can accommodate me."

"You've got a decent set of pipes on you, my girl. The alto baronesses are gonna love you. Follow me."

Diana linked arms with Simon. The best friendships were ones you could pick up after a long gap.

They walked into Westminster Hall. Simon had a prestigious role on the parliamentary estates staff. While he wasn't in charge of Big Ben, he was the closest thing to a caretaker that it had. But this evening, he wasn't taking her skywards but down into the depths of the Palace of Westminster.

The Chapel of St Mary Undercroft was a peculiar feature of the Palace. It had been built in the thirteenth century and then, over the centuries, been used as storage, as a dining room and, allegedly, as stables for Oliver Cromwell's horse. More recently it had been restored for use as a chapel, decorated in sumptuous ecclesiastic style.

Diana followed Simon down the steps into the chapel and admired the arched ceiling, the stained glass and the tiled floor. The space was on the right side of gaudy, but only just.

The room was busy, members of the Parliament Choir milling around. The group met weekly and was open to anyone who worked within the Palace of Westminster (plus the occasional guest stiffener). Diana had joined them a few times in the past, observing the interactions of the politicians. She found it heartening to see them sing together across the Parliamentary divide.

A woman circulated, thrusting paper into people's hands.

"I have to look at the broom cupboard," Diana whispered to Simon. It was a ritual of hers.

She stepped over to the cupboard door. Emily Wilding Davison, the suffragette, had spent the night there during the 1911 census. It had meant she could say her address was the House of Commons, and claim the same rights as a man, when they conducted the census.

"Can you imagine hiding all night in a broom cupboard?" Simon whispered.

Diana looked at the brass plaque on the inside of the door. "All too easily. You have to hand it to old Emily."

She ran her fingers over the gleaming plaque. *So the cleaners even get down here.*

"I must go join the basses." Simon hurried away.

The choir's director took his position at the steps to the altar. Victor Nicholls was a tall man with an expressive, angular face. "Good evening, everybody."

Murmured greetings. Diana slipped in beside the other sopranos, recognising a couple and exchanging silent greetings.

"Warm-ups," said Victor. "Everybody stand tall, shoulders relaxed. Breathe with me for a moment."

Diana followed the warm-up, enjoying the chance to exercise her voice. As they sang, the chapel also seemed to warm up, finding its echoes and its reverberation. The sound was beautiful, melancholic.

Diana frowned. The image of Florence Breecher, dead, was playing in her mind. She glanced over at the altos and at Hanna O'Grady, the Serjeant at Arms, now wearing an informal suit.

Victor called the warm-ups to an end.

"Good evening, choir. Tonight, we embark on a musical journey through Rachmaninoff's Vespers. This masterpiece is known for its ethereal beauty and deep spiritual resonance. I would like us to embrace its emotional depth and bring it to life."

He paused, his eyes flitting over the choir.

"In these rehearsals, my aim is twofold," he continued. "First, we must master the technical intricacies. Each voice has a part to play in creating a unified, transcendent sound. Secondly, I want us to delve into the soul of the music, to express its profound emotions."

The choir members were nodding. Diana had told Zaf that she'd sung backing vocals on hit records and she hadn't been lying. But the discipline involved in singing rock and punk vocals was very different to that required for choral work.

Victor looked around, meeting the eyes of each choir member.

"Let's tackle the opening section."

As the choir members found their starting positions and took a collective breath, Victor raised his hands. Haunting melodies filled the rehearsal space.

Victor drew them to a close after a few minutes and gave out some pointers and instructions.

"Nice to have you back, Diana," whispered Claire, the soprano beside her. "The Honourable Member for South Yardley doesn't have your range."

Diana nodded thanks.

Victor cleared his throat. "Sopranos, do not overpower the altos. Yours are delicate and demure voices here. Basses, let's spend some time working on the *Blagoslovi, dushe moya, Gospoda* section. Pay attention to the sustained low notes and the expressive phrases. Everyone else take five."

The female singers retired to the back, where palace catering had left urns of tea, coffee and jugs of drinking water.

"Delicate and demure," said soprano Claire.

"Nothing delicate or demure about us," Diana commented.

Hanna O'Grady leaned her walking stick against the wall and poured herself a glass of water. Diana decided it was time to approach the Serjeant at Arms with her evidence.

# Chapter Twenty-Five

"Hanna," said Diana. "I wanted to say hello."

The Serjeant at Arms put down the water jug and gave her a blank look. "Hello?"

"Diana Bakewell. I was here yesterday. Right in the Chamber when the... when Florence Breecher was murdered."

"Yes. Tragic. Did you know her?"

"I'm getting to know her better." Diana tightened her grip on Tabitha's folder. "I had things to tell the police."

"I assume they've interviewed everyone who was there."

"Including you?" Diana asked.

Hanna pulled back. "I spoke to the police, yes. In my role at Serjeant at Arms."

"But you were there, weren't you?"

Hanna's frown deepened. "Not at the time. I came as soon as I could, but..." She gave a joyless laugh and pointed at her walking stick. "I don't move all that fast."

"The Palace must be difficult to navigate with a disability."

Another grunted laugh. "My leg is all but mended, but the

cane can be handy when I want to remind people to get out of the way. I'm *not* disabled."

"Altos," the music director called. "Let's work on the challenging section starting at measure twenty-five."

"I have to go," said Hanna.

"Aiming for perfect synchronization," Victor continued as the singers moved about. "We need a seamless blend of voices."

The basses ambled over and helped themselves to refreshments.

"You upsetting our Serjeant at Arms?" Simon asked Diana.

"Me? I—"

He grinned. "Don't worry. She always looks like that."

Diana raised an eyebrow. "By the way, I have a favour to ask."

"Another favour?" he said, a twinkle in his eye.

"I've got a tour group of students from Yorkshire this week. Can we come and see you for a look round the Elizabeth Tower?"

Simon smiled. "You know I love taking kids round, much more fun than the adults. Give me a bell and we'll set it up."

Diana smiled and followed the choir director's instructions to reassemble.

"Sopranos, watch yourself this time," said Victor. "Focus on your vowel placement, altos. Crystal-clear diction."

For another hour, they worked through the piece. Whether it was the rehearsal space or the singing, Diana found herself immersed. It was good to focus on something, to be distracted from thoughts of poor Florence.

Victor drew them to a stop. "Syncopation and precision of timing, everyone." He checked his watch. "Which will have to wait until next week."

It had been a while since Diana had sung in a group, and it

felt good. She wasn't the only one who seemed more relaxed than when they'd arrived. Groups broke away and she heard talk of finding a place to get a drink.

She fell into step beside Hanna O'Grady as the choir made its way out through Westminster Hall.

"Hanna, if I can bother you a second…?"

"Oh, bother away, Mrs…?"

Had Hanna really forgotten?

"Diana. Bakewell. The tour guide. It's just this business with Florence and John Chapman-Moore—"

"What has it to do with Mr Chapman-Moore?"

"The whole case might be linked to his, um, well his interests outside parliament."

"Interests?"

"His…" Diana cursed herself. What was she going to say? She had no proof of any of it.

Hanna O'Grady eyed her. "I do hope you're not about to make some wild accusations about a sitting Member of Parliament."

"Not necessarily wild," Diana said.

"People start baseless rumours. Even researchers like Miss Breecher, though I never met her, are capable of flights of fancy. Did she… did she say anything before she died?"

Diana frowned. "No. Why? What would she have said?"

"Nothing at all, I imagine."

Diana looked down at her folder of evidence. She wasn't going to be giving it to the Serjeant at Arms, she decided. The woman might be in a position of authority but…

What was it about her? Something that made Diana feel she couldn't be trusted.

"No." She fell back to let the woman walk ahead.

Diana clutched the folder as she took the District Line tube from Westminster Station to Victoria. There was a busker in the tunnel to the stairs, playing an old Kinks song on a possibly even older guitar. His voice echoed off the tiled walls with a soulful melancholy that made her think of Rachmaninoff's choral work.

Upstairs, the station concourse was busy. A young woman wearing a leather jacket over a short summer dress stood in front of the information board, holding a single long-stemmed red rose.

Diana approached her with a smile. "Been stood up?"

"Edgar's not answering my messages," the woman replied, still scanning the space for her date.

"Waiting a while?"

"Since eight."

Diana sucked her teeth. "Sounds like he's not coming. Blind date?"

"Dating app."

"Luck of the draw, sometimes." With a sad smile, Diana left the woman to it.

*London*, she thought. Always some drama happening somewhere.

## Chapter Twenty-Six

Diana left her flat early on Wednesday, giving time for a few minutes in the square before walking to work. She took a bin bag, a small handbrush and a pair of strong gloves, and made her circuit. The buildings in Eccleston Square were Georgian, part of a conservation area. Buildings were painted in regulation colours, with alterations that might spoil the grand, uniform design not permitted.

While the council might keep an eye on the fabric of the buildings, a number of them seemed to be empty. Investment properties, no doubt. But it made for untidy gardens.

Diana pulled weeds from the front garden of one of the empty houses, and pushed the bulging pile of post and flyers fully through the letterbox. She brushed the build-up of city dust away from the railings and tried to make the building look like it was cared for.

There was CCTV, presumably a security firm hired to protect the investment. Diana always gave the cameras a little wave, daring them to come out and challenge what she was doing, but nobody ever did. She'd planted seeds in a neglected window box a few days earlier, and already they were germinating. When she got home, she'd go back with her watering can.

There was movement over by the square's garden.

Diana looked through the railings to see a neighbour working her way along with secateurs. "Morning, Nichola."

The woman looked up, gesturing at the flowers she was tending. "Looking grand, isn't it, Diana?"

"It is."

"Popping in for a natter?" Nichola waggled a large tartan thermos flask.

Diana checked her watch. "Probably not, but the weather's good all week, I'll stop by another day."

"Here's a little something for you," Nichola said. "I had to cut back one of the climbing roses with all of its flowers on. Breaks my heart when they're in full bloom."

She reached through the railings to pass Diana a flower. It was white, fringed with a deep, pinkish red. Perfect.

"That's a Dinktrout variety," Nichola said. "Very rare."

"Thank you."

Diana popped it into the buttonhole of her blazer, trying not to think about Paul Kensington's plans to swap it for a horrible corporate fleece. She gave Nichola a wave and walked on.

She surveyed the row of houses to see what else might require her attention. One house had scaffolding, either for painting or repairs. The remaining houses stood in a neat, precise row, testament to the original design. The buildings were approaching their two hundredth birthday. Diana wondered how the occasion might be celebrated.

They'd been built by Queen Camilla's great-great-great-grandfather, Thomas Cubitt. Would Camilla accept an invitation to a party? Would she sit in the gardens, eating canapés with the King and making small talk about the maintenance of render or Portland stone?

This was the London that Diana loved. You could dig into any corner of the city and find unexpected, delicious connections. The square was its own village, but sometimes that village extended right across the capital.

She picked up some litter and pushed it down into her bag as she moved around the square. Once her circuit was complete her day could begin, with everything in good shape.

Heading to work, she passed through Victoria Station and glanced at the spot where the young woman had been waiting last night. Now, in the same spot, was a young man, tall and gawky in a red lumberjack shirt. The confused and pitiful look on his face was an almost perfect match for the woman's yesterday.

Again, Diana couldn't resist. She walked over.

His gaze was locked on the rose in her buttonhole. "Anastasia?"

"Er, no," said Diana. "Are you waiting for a young woman in a leather jacket?"

"Are you her mum?"

Diana laughed. "When were you supposed to meet?"

"Eight o'clock." He pointed at the information boards.

"One of you is twelve hours out." Diana slid the rose from her buttonhole and passed it to him. "I suggest checking your messages, saying you're sorry and giving her this."

"We said eight in the morning," he insisted.

She shrugged. "Sorry goes a long way, Edgar."

## Chapter Twenty-Seven

Zaf was woken by someone tapping his arm.

"Hey, what do you think you're doing?"

Zaf grunted. Where was he?

"Hey, I'm talking to you! What d'you think you're doing?"

"Wait." Zaf forced his eyes open. "Wait. I'm getting up." He blinked. "Newton?"

Newton Crombie stood in the centre aisle of the top deck, hands on hips. "Of course it's Newton! It's my bus!"

Zaf pushed himself up. It wasn't Newton's bus, it was Chartwell and Crouch's bus. But he didn't think pointing that out would help.

"Have you drooled on that seat?" Newton snapped.

Zaf put a hand to his face. "I'll clean the seat, mate, alright? Hang on and let me join the fully-awake club, yeah?"

Newton stood in a simmering silence while Zaf crowbarred himself up and tried to wipe any tell-tale dribble from his face.

"I understand why you're upset, Newton."

"Upset?"

"I'm sorry. I know the bus is your pride and joy. To be

honest, the bus seats out in the garage were so comfy when I napped on them yesterday that I thought I'd try out the ones on the bus. I got here an hour ago and just fell asleep."

"Liar!" shouted Newton. "I know you've spent the night here."

"No, I—"

"I've got it all on camera."

"What?"

"I should tell Paul Kensington."

"No! Don't do that. Look, I'm sorry. I won't do it again, but please don't report me."

Newton looked sceptical. Zaf knew the driver wasn't a fan of the depot manager, but he *was* emotionally attached to the bus.

"Let me clean up and do any other polishing the old girl needs," Zaf said. "I didn't mean any harm." He frowned. "How come the camera was pointing this way? You set it up for your cat monitoring experiment, not for the bus."

Newton's expression softened. "The camera got knocked. It's a bit weird out there. I might need your help with the cat situation."

"Help how?"

"If I don't turn you in for sleeping on the bus, can you help me manage what's going on out here?"

"Of course." Zaf had no idea what Newton was talking about.

Newton stood aside for Zaf to get up and the two of them walked off the bus.

"Wow." Zaf could see what Newton had meant by *the cat situation*.

"It's been a little too successful," Newton said.

"Wow," Zaf repeated.

There had to be at least twenty of them. Maybe fifty. Tabbies. Gingers. A flat-faced long-haired white thing. More than a couple of sleek black things that had to have been panthers in their previous lives. Collared and uncollared, ragged and well-kept, the cats ranged from little more than kittens to a sprawling rug-like thing that Zaf felt was surely half-wildcat.

"I put some food out for my Gus," said Newton.

"Gus?"

Newton pointed at the heavy-set tabby cat they'd spotted on camera. "Gus."

"What was the stuff you put out for them?" asked Zaf. "Cat heroin?"

"I got a bag of sardines from the fish place on Marylebone High Street. They gave me a good price if I agreed to take everything they had left at closing time, so I did. It looked like the sort of stuff a cat might like." He sighed. "Turns out it was."

"There are so many, though. How many? I've never seen so many cats in one go."

Newton tried to count them and gave up. Then he tried counting a sample and multiplying it up, but in the end he shrugged. "More than thirty, less than a hundred. What do I do with them?"

"Surely they'll go away when the food's gone?" Zaf said.

"The food must have gone hours ago. They're still here."

"It's weird the way they stare at you." Zaf looked at Newton, trying to work out what it was about him that fascinated the cats. "It's like you're a cat god or something."

"Power of sardines." Newton gave a small shrug and sniffed his fingers. "Paul won't be pleased."

"He will not," Zaf said. "Look, let me go splash some water

on my face, then I'll get some brooms and maybe we can chase them out of here."

"Good idea. Wait. Why *were* you sleeping on the bus last night? Were you out partying? You're not drunk, are you?"

Zaf opened his mouth, ready with his prepared excuse, then changed his mind. Newton might not be a friend, but he was a decent human being.

He looked down. "I'm... I'm homeless."

"Homeless how?"

"Homeless as in I don't have a home. You know I broke up with Malachi at the weekend?"

"I heard."

"I'd been staying at his, the last few weeks. Pretty much since I got to London. And then when we split... He offered to let me stay. But I was angry and I wanted to flounce out the door and I did and..." He sighed, his stomach clenching. "I'm homeless, Newton, and I can't find anywhere I can afford to stay."

"London rent prices are high."

"Astronomical. This is a great job, but even a single room in a flat costs over a grand a month. There are car parking spaces that cost more in rent than I can afford."

Saying it out loud brought home to Zaf just how bleak his situation was. "I walked all Sunday night, upset. I stayed up partying Monday night with the Foxwood Grange kids, just so I didn't have to go find somewhere to sleep. And last night..." He gestured at the bus. "It was so comfy. I didn't have anywhere else to go."

Newton nodded in understanding. "You can't stay here. You know that."

"I know. I could go back to Birmingham but it wouldn't be fair on my sister, Connie. She says I can stay there any time, but she doesn't want me cluttering up her place again. And going back there would feel like... giving up. I want to make a success of London."

"I'd offer to let you stay with us, but there's barely enough room for me and Siobhan and the little Crombies."

"No, I get it," Zaf said. "I wouldn't ask. Let me go get washed and I'll help out here."

Zaf slipped off to the staff toilets. He retrieved the duffel bag full of his stuff that he'd hidden in the cleaning cupboard, and made himself as presentable as possible.

When he emerged, Newton was already walking around, trying to drive the cats away with the wide end of a broom. He waved it about, making sharp animalistic noises. The cats were ignoring him.

"Is it performance art?" said Diana.

Zaf jumped. He turned to her, standing between him and the door-within-a-door.

"It's complicated." Was he talking about Newton and the cats, or himself?

"Come on," she said. "You look like you could do with a cup of tea."

"I promised I'd help Newton first."

"OK, but then a cup of tea. There's something I want to show you before we pick up our tour party."

## Chapter Twenty-Eight

Diana had a cup of tea waiting in the depot kitchen for Zaf. It was a big spotty mug and she'd heaped in three spoons of sugar because he looked like he needed it.

"Success with the cats?" she asked.

"If you mean, have we successfully danced around the depot with brooms like a pair of prize lemons and not encouraged a single cat to leave the premises then, yes, a complete success."

She wrinkled her nose. "Maybe Newton could get one of the former mayor's sparrowhawks in to scare them away."

"There's so many of them, they'd probably scare the sparrowhawk away." Zaf opened the folder on the table. "What's this?"

Diana glanced at it. "Florence Breecher's evidence on Chapman-Moore's dodgy dealings. The folder Tabitha Welkin gave me yesterday."

Zaf sniffed it. "That smell."

"I know. It's like Westminster Palace infuses everything."

"I thought you were gonna speak to someone yesterday. The whole choir stiffening thing."

Diana sat down opposite him. "I was going to present it to the Serjeant at Arms." She paused. "But there was something about her manner I didn't like."

"Like what?"

"She asked me if Florence had said anything before she died. It was almost as if she expected there to be something. And then when I said I'd seen her in the Commons Chamber right after Florence's death, she flat-out denied it."

"So, she's a bit dodgy herself."

"Maybe. But she'd be keen to bury anything untoward, to protect Parliament's reputation."

Zaf nodded and slurped his tea.

"And d'you remember what O'Grady and Chapman-Moore were arguing about when we first went to his office?" Diana said.

Zaf shrugged. "Doors, wasn't it? Rooms and doors."

Diana nodded. She pulled out the first few top sheets. "These are all to do with properties in London."

"Rooms and doors," said Zaf. "She knew already."

"Possibly."

He slurped his tea again. "They're both dodgy. Dodgy together, even?"

"Also possible. I need time to study this later."

"I'll help."

Diana made an appreciative noise. "Maybe you can come over to mine for that tea and sympathy I promised."

"Oh, that sounds great." His face brightened.

"But *that's* not what I wanted to show you," she said.

"No?"

"I was thinking about love on the way here."

Zaf gave a cynical laugh. "Well, you're never too old to get back on that horse, Diana, and—"

"Not me, you daft boy. Love generally. It makes fools of people. It knows no reason."

"Tell me about it."

"Our Mr Chapman-Moore was, as you put it, a well-known philanthropist. A lothario."

"A sexual predator," Zaf said.

"Most likely," said Diana. "He's been like that his whole life. Since Leeds, Azar told you."

"Yup." Zaf slurped some more tea. Diana watched him, trying to ignore the sound.

"And our student guest, Ava," she said, "she's been showing quite an interest in him."

"I've no idea what a young person could see in that man."

"Apart from the wealth and the power, you mean."

Zaf made a disgusted noise.

"Foxwood Estate Agents," Diana said. "That was what his business up north was called. DCI Sugarbrook mentioned it in passing. He sold it before he made his permanent move south."

"If you say so."

She put her phone on the table and flicked to the website she'd found on her walk from Victoria. She turned the phone towards Zaf.

Zaf leaned in. "Old newspaper article."

Diana nodded. It was twenty years old at most; to Zaf, that would be ancient.

"Big changes for Foxwood Estate Agents," Zaf read. "That's John Chapman-Moore in the photo. With hair. I'll admit he had a certain papa bear charm then."

"Look at who's next to him."

Zaf's gaze flicked across the screen.

"Look where his arm is," Diana suggested.

Zaf's finger hovered over the young woman with the frizzy blonde hair. "OK," he said. "She looks kind of familiar, I guess." His gaze dropped to the caption below and the list of names. "Emma Franks. Wait. No."

Diana smiled at his shocked expression. "Ava told us her mum had worked at an estate agent. It didn't occur to us it might be that one."

Zaf's brow creased. "Hang on. So, John Chapman-Moore was having an affair with Ava's mum back in the day."

"Possibly. But—"

"Ava's the only one who knew anything about him. More than a tad obsessed, really. Not total psycho cray-cray, but definitely obsessed."

Diana watched as the pieces slotted together in Zaf's mind. "And what you said about Ava when she left his office..." she prompted.

"Her hand under her jacket. Hiding something." Zaf gasped. "She took the knife! She wanted to kill him because of what he did to her mum."

Diana tutted. "Not the knife."

"The cup?"

"The cup. The cup she dropped when she went to help Florence."

Diana watched the realisation dawn on Zaf's face. It was a beautiful thing to see.

"DNA," he said.

"DNA."

"His saliva on the cup. She wanted to do a paternity test. Like on the TV shows. '*Is this MP your baby daddy?*'"

"That's my guess," Diana said. "It's fanciful, but she is a teenager."

Zaf sat back, stunned.

"You said he was old enough to be her dad," Diana told him. "I'm thinking he's exactly old enough to be her dad."

"This is crazy."

Diana looked at the clock on the kitchen wall. "And now we need to pick them up and take them on a tour of Big Ben." She took their cups to the sink.

"But will we tell her?" Zaf asked. "I mean, should we confront her?"

"That's a big question," Diana said. "And I'm not sure I know the answer."

# Chapter Twenty-Nine

Diana waited until the school group was on board the bus before she shared her news. "I'm pleased to tell you that this morning we've been invited to look inside the Elizabeth Tower."

Zaf chimed in. "You'll remember that the Elizabeth Tower is Big Ben's Sunday name."

"Sunday name?" asked Ethan.

"It's the name your mom uses for telling you off. You can have a nickname that everyone uses, but if your mom calls you by your proper name then you know you're in trouble."

There was some positive-sounding chatter from the students, suggesting that Big Ben was a popular choice. Zaf moved around them, poring over phones with them.

Diana resisted pointing out that Big Ben was actually the bell inside the tower. There'd be time enough for that during the tour.

Newton set off down Baker Street, passing Grosvenor Square with its regal embassies on his way south.

Zaf took the microphone as they drove through Piccadilly Circus. "You'll recognise The Ritz from off the telly. It was in the film Notting Hill – my mom loves that one."

Newton turned off towards St James' Square.

"So this place here, St James' Square, is interesting," Zaf said. "There are a fair few private members' clubs here. No women allowed in historically, still not in some of them. And as for people like me…" He frowned out of the window. "They were a place where men would meet, talk and have their meals prepared for them."

"Sounds perfect!" Ethan called out.

"Shut up, Ethan," muttered Ava.

Zaf continued. "Most of the buildings don't have signs up. Probably deliberate."

"But they can't still ban women, can they?" asked a girl. "That's sexist."

Diana gave a grim smile. "There are still places women aren't allowed to enter."

"Here? Places here, in *actual England*?" Ava asked as they circled the square and headed back along Pall Mall.

Diana nodded. "Many have opened their doors to women, and there are spaces women have set up to redress the balance. But they're private clubs, so the laws don't apply in the same way they do for public facilities." She winked. "And the dinosaurs need somewhere they can relax, don't they?"

They took a right at Trafalgar Square and headed down Whitehall towards Parliament.

"I'll be back for you later," Newton said.

"Cats to chase with brooms?" Zaf suggested.

Newton looked ahead, out of the windscreen, his expression grim.

The Palace of Westminster was still closed to the public,

but Simon Smallchild met them outside once they'd been through security. He strolled up and down, greeting everyone in the group with a handshake and a whiskery grin.

"My good friend Diana has asked me to show you our beautiful clock tower." He had the manner of an old-style schoolmaster: Diana imagined him swishing a black cape as he spoke. "I am therefore privileged to take you on a highly irregular and very much unscheduled visit. Buckle in, everyone, you've got a good many steps to climb. If anyone has concerns about the climb then please make yourselves known now. I regret to say that this tour is not suitable for those who are less mobile."

"How many steps is a good many?" asked Zaf, looking concerned.

"There are three hundred and thirty-four altogether, but we won't do them all in one go," said Simon.

Simon led them across New Palace Yard to the tower. He unlocked the door and took them inside to the staircase.

"We will start climbing in just a moment," he said. "But first, look up at the rather nice pattern of the stairs spiralling up, up and away. We recently carried out an extensive programme of restoration work on this magnificent building, so it's in excellent shape. The tower now looks very much as envisaged by Pugin, the architect who designed it back in the eighteen forties."

He turned to beam at the group. The students muttered and shuffled their feet. He shrugged and turned to begin the climb.

Diana took the lead with Simon while Zaf followed behind, at the rear of the group. The white-painted stairs seemed fine for the first few flights, but soon Diana's legs began to burn with the effort. Diana considered herself a woman with stamina though, so she kept going.

"Are we there yet?" came a plaintive cry from behind.

"Are you counting the steps?" asked Simon. "We're a quarter of the way to the clock faces."

The group fell quiet, huffing and grunting taking the place of chatter as they concentrated on getting up the stairs. After what seemed an impossible number of steps, Simon led them away from the stairs and through a doorway. They followed through into a narrow walkway.

"Single file, spread out along here and we'll talk about the clock faces when the whole group has arrived," called Simon.

Diana watched the faces of the students as they realised that they were behind the famous clock face. Standing behind the glass, with sunlight streaming through from outside, the numerals were clearly visible and almost human-sized.

"All here?" boomed Simon. "Now, I don't suppose you've seen this view of Big Ben before."

"In that film," said a lad. "Where they're hanging off the clock handles."

"Ah, the 1978 version of *The Thirty-Nine Steps*."

"No. The one with Jackie Chan."

Simon was unfazed. "*Shanghai Knights*. 2003. Yes. So, let's take a look at one of Pugin's clock faces, shall we? Many clock faces will have the number four represented by IIII, but Pugin decided that he preferred IV. Even more remarkable is his decision to do away with the X for the number ten and use the letter F instead. You'll see it on other clocks around the parliamentary estate."

"How big are the hands?" asked a girl.

"The minute hand is four point two metres," replied Simon.

Zaf was further down the line, pointing at the phone in Ethan's hand. Diana leaned over to take a look. She nudged Simon. "Zaf's translating for the students who aren't familiar with analogue clock faces."

Simon smiled and raised his voice again. "I have been reminded that this type of clock face hails from the pre-digital era, which means that many of you won't have grown up with it. If we take a slow walk around the tower I'll explain it to you."

Simon led them through the history and the recent restoration of the clock faces while explaining how the time was marked. He held up a hand as they returned to the stairs.

"Now, we want to see the famous bell at the moment when it strikes. We should get a move on if we're going to get there in time."

He led them up more stairs and they emerged into the windy belfry, where they climbed a narrower staircase to look down on the bells.

Simon pointed downwards. "When the bells strike the hour, you will hear the different notes they create to make up the Westminster chime. Then Big Ben's hammer will strike eleven times to tell everyone that it's eleven o'clock."

The students' eyes were fixed on the bells.

"I will pass around ear defenders," said Simon. "Don't remove them until I signal to you that the sequence is complete."

They all put on the ear defenders, some of the students looking reluctant. They waited in silence for the bells to sound.

Zaf pointed at each bell as it played, encouraging the students to do the same. The game was popular, and they all tried to time when the Great Bell would strike.

"Too early!" Zaf laughed. They'd all pointed a moment too

soon. Diana smiled as she watched him, pleased that his dull mood in the kitchen earlier had lifted.

When the tune was over, they all cheered each other and removed the ear defenders.

"Great job everyone," Zaf yelled. "We could all get jobs as Big Ben impersonators. Bong!"

# Chapter Thirty

As they descended the steps, Diana's phone buzzed: a message.

"Newton's delayed," she told Zaf. "Technical issues, he says."

"Technically too many cats in the depot for one man to cope with?"

Diana looked up at the cloudless sky. "We've got plenty of time. A pleasant walk back to the hotel would be good."

"Did you say more walking?" a boy groaned.

Moans came from the school party, the loudest of them from the teachers.

"It's a forty-five-minute walk that-a-way." Diana pointed with her brolly. "And maybe we'll see something exciting on the way."

"Are you saying we will, or we might?" asked Ethan.

"This is London," Diana told him. "There's almost always something exciting to see. For example, our route will take us through St James' Park where, seeing as it's a sunny day, your teachers might decide to buy everyone an ice-crea—"

"School funds are for emergency use only," said Mr Chaplin.

"Overheating kids, that's an emergency, right?" said Zaf.

The park was a fifteen-minute walk from the Palace of Westminster. The sun was warm, and though the teachers were reluctant to splash out on snacks, everyone was happy to sit by the lake and relax.

Or almost everyone, at least.

"Parks are boring unless you've got a football," said Ethan.

"Did you know this park has a bomb disposal facility?" said Diana.

"You make stuff up."

She shook her head. "They did have one here, to handle any bombs found nearby. On Duck Island over there."

Ethan looked over at the buildings on the island in the lake.

"I wonder if it's called Duck Island because of the birds," said Zaf, "or because that's what you need to do if a bomb goes off."

Ethan rolled his eyes and wandered off to join his mates.

Diana turned to Mr Chaplin. "A 99 flake would really do the trick right about now."

He gave her a long look.

"Zaf would like one too. That's right, isn't it Zaf?"

"Absolutely."

Mr Chaplin scowled but turned and walked off in the direction of an ice cream van, pausing to speak to the students.

"Good for him," said Diana, smiling.

"Still not forgiven them for abandoning us on the first day," said Zaf as they watched the two teachers gather up an ice cream order.

Diana nodded. "Total dereliction of duty."

They sat on a bench, side by side. Diana took the folder

Tabitha had given her out of her bag and opened it between them so they could both look through.

"This document's an executive summary of John Chapman-Moore's Helping Hands for the Homeless initiative," Diana said. "It tells us more or less what we knew from what Florence said on the tour. The basic gist of the scheme is that there are lots of people who can't afford housing—"

"Tell me about it," said Zaf.

"—but there are also lots of unoccupied properties in central London. That's true enough near me. Several houses on Eccleston Square have no one in them. The purpose of the bill is to match those up and offer government grant incentives to property owners to open up their spaces for people to move into. It's all laid out here."

"Well that's weird," said Zaf.

"Why? It sounds a good idea."

"Not the idea. The fact that it's described here. Florence knew all of this because she was involved. But if she was putting together a secret file, why would she include an idiot's guide to something she knows perfectly well?"

"Good point," said Diana. "Maybe she'd already decided who she was going to give it to. Maybe she wanted them to have all the background."

"Right." He reached for the diary and flicked through. "Did she have any secret meetings planned?"

"Like a meeting with an investigative journalist?"

"Or the police, if it's that dodgy."

Zaf had the diary open to the final week of Florence Breecher's life. The only things of note were the headings *Tab's Party* and *Hog Club, Berkeley Square*, both written in scrawled block letters.

"Hog Club," said Diana. "I thought I knew every private

members' club in London, but I haven't heard of that one. Mind you, given Florence was something of a party animal, it might be a nightclub."

"I've never heard of it," said Zaf.

Stumped, Diana looked at the next page in the folder. It was a sheet about an apartment complex.

"This is glossy, like it's part of a brochure." She checked the fine print at the end. "It says here that it's taken from an information pack for something called The Fairview New Start building development."

"Right," said Zaf. "Quite a lot of these other documents talk about the Fairview New Start building. There's something called a *fully evidenced strategic proposal*. Whatever that is."

Diana looked at the document. It had the same glossy finish as the information pack, but was much thicker. As she flicked through the pages, she could see that it was some sort of business case.

"So, it's a building over in Bow," she said. "The idea is that homeless people will each be offered a small apartment to get them off the streets." She read further. "This building will house two hundred people, apparently. There are lots of tables and forecasts of its impact. How many people it can house, for how much government money."

"Sounds like a good thing," said Zaf.

She pulled a piece of paper towards her and scanned through it. It was a report from Companies House. "Now this might be relevant." She pushed the paper towards Zaf.

Zaf looked over the page. "It's a company report for Fairview New Start." He shook his head. "This is all gobbledegook to me." He looked at her. "I'm an artist, not a businessman." He shuddered. "Or a politician."

Diana smiled, leaning over to look at the document. "It says the company was incorporated twelve months ago, and we have a list of directors – oh. John Chapman-Moore's one of them."

His name was in the middle of a list of names that meant nothing to Diana, but it was clear Florence had wanted to highlight it. There were asterisks either side of it, each drawn in a continuous line so they looked like little flowers.

"Not the best artwork," Zaf said.

Diana raised an eyebrow. "Don't judge the dead."

'Sorry." He wrinkled his nose, looking over towards the teachers queuing for ice creams.

"I'm getting the shape of this thing," Diana said. "Whether it's a good initiative or not, John Chapman-Moore stands to make a big pile of cash. And he's the one pushing it through Parliament."

"So, he sets up a new law where property owners get grants for providing homes for the homeless. And then he makes sure he's one of them and makes a load of dough."

Diana smirked. She hadn't heard the word *dough* used for a while.

"It's cynical and manipulative," she said, "but not necessarily illegal."

Zaf stuck out his bottom lip. "Florence obviously had her own thoughts on it."

"Maybe we should go check out this Fairview development some—"

Diana stopped as a shadow moved over them. She shielded the sun from her eyes with her hand as she looked up.

The face was familiar. Perhaps more familiar than it had been a few days ago.

She closed the dossier and recognised the face.

"Oh. Hello, Ava."

# Chapter Thirty-One

Zaf couldn't help but look at Ava in a new light now, wondering if he could see any of John Chapman-Moore in her face. Ava pointed back across the green lawn of St James' Park.

"Some of the lads want to know if they can paddle in the pond," she said.

Zaf looked across at the long lake that cut through the park.

"They want to know if they can go jump in a lake?" he said.

"I told them they were morons, but I thought we needed a professional opinion."

Diana scanned the area around them. "Are your teachers not about?"

"Still queuing up for ice creams, I think."

Diana looked over towards the ice cream van: no sign of the teachers. She gritted her teeth and looked back at Ava.

"In that case, no," she said, "tell your friends they can't jump in the lake. I'm not jumping in to save them."

Ava shrugged and turned away.

"Ava?" Diana said.

"Yes?" The girl turned back.

She blinked up at the girl then said, "Is John Chapman-Moore your father?"

Ava's cheeks flushed. "Who... who told you?"

"It's OK," said Diana. "We're the only ones who know, I think."

The girl was breathing hard. Not quite hyperventilating, but not far off. Zaf hoped he wouldn't have to use the first-aid training provided by Paul Kensington.

"I mean, I don't even know. I thought... I mean, I thought..." Her shoulders slumped. "How did you know?"

"The cup. Your questions." Diana shrugged. "We worked it out. Did your mum tell you he was your dad?"

"My mum's dead."

"Sorry," Zaf said.

"That's very sad," Diana added.

"She wasn't well for a long time. She drank. She didn't tell me. Dom – her most recent boyfriend, my stepdad I guess – he cared for her at the end. We still live in the same place, him and me. He's alright. A bit of div. Dom. Daft Old Man, I call him. But you can't pick who you live with, can you?"

She was calming, coming down from the panic. Zaf was relieved; he wasn't sure what the procedure was for a hyperventilating teenage tour member.

"I just wanted to know," Ava said. "To be able to meet my real dad and look him in the eye."

"And if Chapman-Moore is your real dad...?" Diana asked.

"I'm not sure I want anything to do with him. He's the epitome of the self-serving politician."

"Epitome." Zaf smiled. "Good word."

Diana gave her a smile. "You are one of the most intelligent young people I've had the pleasure to meet. I hope that doesn't sound condescending."

"No." Ava looked down at the gravel in front of the bench.

"And," Diana said, "if you're not happy with the self-serving politician representing Pudsey and Otley, you'll be eighteen soon enough."

"Old enough to vote him out," Zaf said.

"Or stand for his seat," added Diana.

Ava looked up. She frowned, then pointed back towards the other students again. "I'd better tell them not to jump in the lake."

"Someone has to," Diana said, her voice gentle.

Ava walked away as the teachers appeared around a hedge with two students in two, the four of them carrying a round of ice creams between them. Mr Chaplin approached with two 99 flakes and handed them to Zaf and Diana.

"Cheers," said Zaf. Diana took hers without a word, her gaze on Ava.

Once they'd all eaten – and no one had fallen in the lake – Zaf and Diana stood up.

"Can you do the honours?" Diana asked.

He nodded, eying her brolly. They wouldn't need it, he hoped.

"Come on, you lot. Back to the hotel!"

The students followed, laughing and tossing ice cream wrappers towards bins. He reminded them to pick up the ones that had missed, and at last they reached the edge of the park.

Diana put up her brolly, both to protect herself from the hot sun and to give them something to follow. The crossed the Mall and skirted along the eastern edge of Green Park, where people lay in the sun on stripey deckchairs. As they crossed Piccadilly, Diana stopped.

"Oh, my goodness!"

Zaf took hold of her elbow and steered her across a pedestrian crossing, convinced she was about to get hit by a black cab. "What is it?"

"Daft Old Man."

"Who is?"

"Dom. Ava's step-dad."

"And?"

Diana's face hardened. She waved her brolly. "This way."

She turned left then right, taking them up Half Moon Street and along Curzon Street.

Zaf followed, puzzled. "You going to tell me what this is about?"

"A hunch," said Diana. "A troubling answer."

"OK," he said, still confused.

They came out into Berkeley Square, full of grand houses, swanky restaurants and even a sports car showroom. Zaf peered over towards it, amazed at how much money some Londoners had.

"Wait here." Diana dashed into a nameless building with tall Georgian windows.

The students gathered around Ethan, the two teachers dawdling at the rear.

"Where's she gone?" Ethan asked.

Zaf was ready with an answer. "Important tour guide business."

Diana emerged a few minutes later with a triumphant look on her face. With a wave of her brolly, she led them around the square and out into Bruton Street.

"You gonna tell me now?" Zaf whispered to her.

"It wasn't Hog Club," Diana told him, not breaking pace. "In Florence's diary."

"No?"

"It was H.O.G. club."

"Is that a place?"

She gestured over her shoulder. "That back there is one of the small but growing number of private members clubs just for women. It's a lovely place. An amazing library in there. World-class."

How did she get access to these places?

"Yeah?" Zaf said.

"And Hanna O'Grady is a member. I just checked."

"Hanna. The Serjeant at Arms?" Zaf hurried to keep up with Diana's walking pace. She wasn't normally this impatient. "H.O.G. is Hanna O'Grady." His grin turned to a frown. "So, the night before she was murdered, Florence went to see Hanna O'Grady at her club."

"Exactly. A secret rendezvous," Diana replied, glancing up. "Which is particularly interesting because as well as denying that she was in the Chamber at the time of the murder, Hanna was keen to tell me she'd never met Florence. She made a point of it."

Zaf thought of the folder. "Florence went to her with her evidence and Hanna turned her away and then... Wow. The next day, she was dead."

Diana raised both eyebrows, then her brow furrowed. "But the folder isn't evidence of anything criminal, not that I can see."

"So you reckon Hanna could have killed her to silence her. Why?"

Diana looked around, checking to see if any of the students were listening. The group trailed behind, caught up in their own conversations.

She looked at Zaf. "You're still coming to my place later? For that cup of tea."

"I am."

"Good," she said. "We need to work out what we're going to do."

## Chapter Thirty-Two

The return journey to their Marylebone hotel took them up New Bond Street and across Oxford Street. Several students squealed with delight when they spotted the Disney Store, and begged to be allowed to look around. Diana sighed, then acquiesced.

She and Zaf stood outside, waiting and watching the crowds of shoppers.

"D'you get angry that you show people the historic sights of London but all they get excited for is buying a plush Mickey Mouse?" Zaf asked.

"People are people," Diana said. "I'm confident their memories of Big Ben and Westminster will outlast any cuddly toy."

At last the students emerged, some carrying bulging bags. They walked through Mayfair, the students pointing out the boutique shops and the Bentleys. They continued past the chain stores of Oxford Street, back to Baker Street and the Redhouse Hotel.

Penny was waiting for them at the reception desk, smiling.

"Parliament's open again tomorrow. You can take your visitors. And Mr Chapman-Moore rang, says he's expecting to see you again, early afternoon."

"He called you himself?" Diana asked.

"Well, no. His friend did it, the other MP."

"Azar," Zaf said, amazed that Chapman-Moore was already treating the man as his new assistant.

Diana turned to the two teachers. "I think that works. A relaxed morning and a late start."

"Works for us," said Mrs Swinburn.

"Good," Diana said. "I think we're all very keen to meet Mr Chapman-Moore once again." She nodded at the teachers, and she and Zaf stepped outside, making for the bus depot.

"Ooh, you said that in a cold voice," Zaf said as they walked.

"Did I?" she said.

"Oh, yeah. Like *'Mr Chapman-Moore, we'd like a word with you.'* Sort of like you're ready for a smackdown."

"I'm not sure what that is."

"You know, like in wrestling."

Diana gave him a look. "You learn something new every day."

As they entered the Chartwell and Crouch depot, Zaf spotted Newton, gesturing wildly towards the cats that still milled about the place.

"How's it all going?" Zaf asked.

"Is it me or are there even more cats than before?" added Diana.

"How can you be so flippant?" Newton said. "This is very stressful. I've even had to lie to Paul Kensington to keep him away."

"Newton, I don't believe that for a second. You're as pure as the driven snow."

"Is this what it takes for you to turn bad?" Zaf said.

Newton shrugged. "Y'know what Paul's like, he'd send for the kitten extermination squad. Probably got them on speed dial."

"So what's happening? Have any of the cats left?" Zaf asked.

"Don't think so. It's not easy to count them, but there seems to be the same amount. I've been trying to build a dossier. Come and see."

"More dossiers," Diana whispered to Zaf as they followed Newton into the kitchen, cats weaving between their legs. A couple of the bolder ones pawed Zaf's calves, looking for attention. He leaned down to scratch the chin of a chunky tortoiseshell.

Newton had stuck photos of cats on the kitchen wall. Labels described each of them in detail. He'd done about twenty.

Zaf read a couple.

*Black and white with green eyes. Paws all white. Possibly a female. Attitude unfriendly.*

*Tabby. Neutered male. Thin. Very tolerant.*

"This is great, Newton," Zaf said. "I like how you've organised them by colour. How d'you know you haven't got two pictures of the same cat, though?"

Newton shrugged. "That's why I am trying to be comprehensive in my descriptions. I had to Google how to tell boy cats and girl cats apart. It seems they're not all that keen for you to look."

Both of Newton's arms were peppered with plasters. There was another on his neck.

Zaf suppressed a smile. "Oh, man. Occupational injuries. Can't you use gloves?"

Newton pointed to a large cat, mostly white with patches of tan and black. It sat on a shelf and chewed on a glove, glaring down at them with pure malevolence.

"That one up there seems to be triggered by gloves. As soon as I pick one up it runs by like some kind of angry whirlwind and grabs it in its mouth. It's eaten at least three since you left."

Zaf stared at the cat. "It's definitely just a normal cat? How do you know it's not from a zoo or something?"

"I need to complete the dossier. Then I can match it against descriptions of cats that are missing in the area."

"You need help?"

"We can stay for a while," Diana said, "but then Zaf's coming to mine for tea and cake."

Newton looked between the two of them. "All help would be appreciated."

"As long as it doesn't involve that one up there, it scares me." Zaf looked up at the glove-eating monster.

Newton fetched his polaroid camera.

"Ooh, you've got one of those that spits the picture straight out," Zaf said. "I always wanted one of them."

"You can have a go with it. I'll position the cat, you take the picture." Newton grabbed a smaller black and white cat and lifted its tail. "I think this one's a girl." He dropped the tail and tried to get the cat to face Zaf.

Zaf shifted sideways, following the cat's movement. "Is this what it's like being paparazzi?"

"Do the noise," Newton said.

"What noise?"

"The cat noise. The one they like. I'm trying not to say it because then they all look at me. We need them to look at you."

Zaf searched his memory for noises that might attract cats.

He whistled. "Like that?"

"That's dogs, you idiot. Stop it. If we get dogs in here too, it'll be bedlam." Newton shook his head. "You want the cat noise."

Zaf tried a kissing noise. Big, wet smackeroos.

Newton growled. "Do you seriously not know the cat noise? *Pspspsps.*"

"*Pspsps?*" Zaf tried. "Oh, yeah. *Pspspsps*, come on then kitties, look at me!"

He snapped a picture of the black and white cat. It was wriggling fiercely, bored of Newton's attention.

"That took long enough," said Newton. "Maybe the next one'll be quicker." He gestured towards the rogues' gallery on the wall. "Let's get this one up there and move on."

## Chapter Thirty-Three

A large tabby pushed against Zaf's legs as he jotted the black and white cat's details onto a label. He reached down to stroke its head. "You're a beautiful colour, aren't you? Are you on the wall yet?"

Newton walked over and stared hard at the cat. "I don't think I've done him... no. You're up next then, Gus."

"Is that... is it the original one?" asked Zaf. "The one who nicked your tuna?"

"He is."

"How d'you know his name?"

Newton shrugged. "He looks like a Gus. Reminds me of Gus Grissom."

"Who?"

Newton gave him a look. "The Apollo astronaut. This cat has the same noble explorer spirit. The white by his ears and under his chin looks just like an astronaut's helmet. This is definitely Gus."

Newton took over fussing Gus so Zaf could take a picture. Zaf looked through the viewfinder, then peered over the top of the camera to check what he was seeing. "Is that cat grinning at me?" he asked. "I swear to God it was grinning. I didn't even make the noise!"

They waited for the photo to develop and made some notes.

"What shall we say about Gus?" Zaf said. "That he's friendly and grins? That he looks like an astronaut? It sounds insane."

"Don't overthink it," said Newton. "There's a lot of cats to do. I might need to go out and get more cat food soon."

"I thought we were hoping they'd go away if there wasn't food here."

"It's not working though, is it? I can't have 'em starving. I think they might have other needs as well." Newton pulled a face. "Toilet needs."

"Oh. How does that work with cats?"

"A litter tray," Newton replied. "I think they might have already nominated Paul Kensington's Japanese zen garden as a stand-in."

"No." Zaf wasn't sure which he felt more, horror or elation. Paul Kensington was a bad boss, everyone knew that, but he was proud of his Japanese Zen garden and spent a lot of time raking patterns in the sand. He insisted that it encouraged mindfulness and helped him make better executive decisions.

"It'll be fine," Newton said. "We'll get them a proper litter tray. Maybe ten of them. Then clean them out before Paul Kensington sees what's happened. He'll never be any the wiser."

Newton made it sound simple. Zaf looked around at the cats that had taken over every surface in the depot. He wasn't so sure.

Diana was equally sceptical. "So all we have to do is keep

Paul Kensington away until we've re-homed dozens of cats, and also restore his Japanese zen garden so he doesn't realise it's been used as a litter tray?"

"Yes," said Newton. "I'll get a fresh bag of sand when I go out for supplies. Why don't I do that now while you carry on with the dossier?"

"I think I'll clean out the zen garden in preparation," Diana said.

"Fine. Right."

"And what was it you said to Paul?" she asked as Newton went to leave. "To keep him away?"

"Gas leak."

Newton walked off to the shops with his string bag, Diana went to explore the horrors that awaited in the zen garden, and Zaf picked the next cat for the dossier wall. He chose it by picking up the camera and looking around until he spotted a cat that was sitting still.

"Good kitty. *Pspsps*." He clicked to take the picture and went to stroke the cat, looking for clues to its temperament. He realised he'd forgotten to ask Newton how to sex a cat. Was this one a boy or a girl? He stared at its face, hoping for a clue, but the cat wasn't about to tell him.

"'Scuse me puss, I need to have a little look under here." He picked up the cat's tail.

In an instant, the cat was transformed from a placid sweetheart into a hissing ball of viciousness. Its fur stood on end and it growled at him, then hissed as it lashed out its claws, raking his arm where he still held its tail.

"Ow!" Zaf howled and snatched his arm away. The scratches weren't deep but they were sore.

He completed the notes for that cat, listing its gender as

unknown and making a note that it didn't like having its tail touched.

The phone on the wall rang.

Zaf hesitated, wondering what to do. He picked it up. "Hello?"

"Ah, finally someone picks up." It was Paul Kensington. "I've been ringing every extension. Who is this, anyway? Your telephone manner needs work."

"It's Zaf. Zaf Williams."

"I phoned to get an update on this gas situation. It's very strange because I called the gas company and they have no record of an incident in this area."

"Oh yeah, that. Newton's liaising with them. It's not the gas company – it's someone else." Zaf put his knuckles in his mouth: *what a daft lie.*

"What on earth do you mean? Like someone has a propane tank that's breached or something?"

"Oh yes! Yes, it's that!" Zaf said, feeling the pressure lift. "Up the road. That's what happened. A propane tank."

"Which company is it? I can phone them for an update. They can't just expect to close down other people's businesses without keeping them informed."

"Err... right. I think that's what Newton's gone to say to them. He'll definitely update you when he knows more."

"He'd better. Why are you there, anyway? Newton told me the bus garage is within the blast radius."

"I'm just leaving now," said Zaf. "Bye!"

He slammed the phone down and looked at it. He hoped he hadn't made things worse. He and Newton would need to compare their versions of the fictional gas leak, keep their stories straight.

# Chapter Thirty-Four

Diana and Zaf got back to her house a little later than planned: not tea-time anymore, but not really evening yet.

They'd left Newton to it back at the depot. The cat problem had brought a certain manic zeal to the driver's face, and taking photos for the identity wall had unlocked the obsessive collector part of his personality. Diana was convinced that if they'd let him, Newton would have had them helping him long past midnight.

Zaf had carted his large duffel bag with him from the depot. Diana didn't know what was in it, and didn't ask. As they entered Eccleston Square, he shifted the bag from one shoulder to the other and looked up at the grand buildings surrounding the beautiful garden.

"You do *not* live here," he said.

"I do."

"Shut up."

"That's mine there. Not the whole thing. I'm the middle floor, Alexsei has the bottom and it's Bryan at the top."

Zaf stood back on the wide pavement, staring up at the building. "London does this weird thing with houses. Yours is like ten Downing Street."

Diana resisted the urge to educate him on the differences between Downing Street's early Georgian architecture and the much more stringent adherence to Greco-Roman classical styles on her square. "How so?"

Zaf stepped further back and framed the house between his hands. "When I used to see Number Ten on the telly, I thought it was a regular terraced house like the ones in Birmingham. It's not though, it's massive. But in a sneaky way. If I was a Hollywood A-lister or a rap star then I'd be straight out to buy a massive house and it would *look* like a massive house. Maybe turrets, maybe a helipad on top. Definitely a huge fence round it. What's weird is just making a terraced house really, really big. Like this one." He waved a hand at the lavish frontage.

Diana smiled. "I see what you mean." She looked up at the elegant facade. Columns flanked the door, a balcony wrapped around the entire row of houses above the ground floor, and iron railings skirted the stairs down to the basement. "If it helps, I'm only in the middle portion of this house. But yes, it's definitely a generous building."

"Generous?" He laughed, turning to the green space beyond the railings opposite. "And you get your own little park."

Diana smiled. "One of the joys of living here. It's our garden. The square's garden."

"The garden belongs to the square? Not the council?"

"It's owned and held in trust for residents. It's beautiful, I can show it to you if you like."

Zaf crossed the road and peered through the railings. "There's a shed in there."

"There are a couple of buildings, it's a big garden. Want to go in?"

"Yeah."

Diana found her keys and opened the gate.

"It's a proper secret garden," Zaf said, stepping inside.

They ambled around the network of little paths. There were shady, secluded nooks and communal areas with barbecue equipment.

"Is that a tennis court?" Zaf asked. "Bloody hell."

"It is. It's such a great space here."

"And the little shed too?"

"For storing gardening equipment, mostly Nichola's. She tends the flowers."

Zaf seemed more taken with the shed than with the tennis court. Perhaps he wasn't a sports fan.

"Something smells nice." Zaf sniffed the air.

"There are lots of scented plants, I think it's jasmine you can smell. There are plenty of edible ones too."

"It's weird to think we're in London. It's so quiet," Zaf said.

"It can be." Diana led him out and up the front steps to her house. Zaf walked in and looked around.

"You must be on a different pay grade to me, Diana. This is mental huge."

"I have a… a favourable rent agreement."

He gave her a frown but she said no more, instead leading him up the sturdy staircase to her first-floor flat.

Diana didn't hold back when it came to interior design, and newcomers to her flat had a range of reactions. Zaf's was muted.

He wandered past the original paintings on her walls,

narrowing his eyes as he took them in. He stopped at the window. "See, this is what I'm talking about. This window is the size of a bus shelter."

"True," she said. "Big windows mean it can get cold here in winter."

He turned and looked at her colourful crochet scarf wall. A friend, obsessed with making the scarves, gave her one each time they met. Diana had decided they were art, and hung them like a fringe from the picture rail.

She spotted a glimmer of a smile on Zaf's face.

"You'd have liked Bryan," she said.

"Bryan?"

She pointed at the high ceiling. "Bryan upstairs. He had a taste for the ridiculous."

"You think I'm ridiculous."

"I think you like beautiful things and have a strong sense of... shall I say, whimsy?"

"I don't know. What's that?"

"Whimsy," she said. "Things that aren't quite the norm."

She went through to the kitchen and put the kettle on. As it boiled Zaf called through from the other room.

"Can I ask a weird favour?"

"Sure."

"The shower's broken at my place. Can I use yours?"

Diana poked her head through the door. "Of course. If the pipes rattle, don't panic. There's towels in the airing cupboard next to the sink."

Zaf all but leapt up and headed for the bathroom with his duffel bag.

"And when you come out you can tell me the story of your break-up with whatsisface," she said.

He was a full half hour in the shower, and emerged beaming and refreshed.

"You are a star, Miss Bakewell." He slid into a chair at the table she'd set out. "Is that lemon drizzle cake?"

"It is."

"That's one of my favourites."

"I must be psychic. Help yourself and I'll pour us some tea."

Zaf ate a slice of the cake. "It's perfect. You bake it yourself?"

"I don't bake," she said. "I *can* but I don't. I'm a big believer in letting experts do their work, and paying them for it."

"So what are you an expert on?" he asked through another mouthful.

"London." Diana leaned in, smiling. "The greatest of cities."

"You ever been to Brum?"

She shook her head. "Reckon it could challenge London to the title of greatest city?"

He wrinkled his nose. "It's like comparing a kitten to a lion, like, er, a donut to a wedding cake. My home city's amazing and a lot of fun, like the best Krispy Kreme donut, but London is something else."

"I believe it is," Diana agreed. "And what's your area of expertise?"

"Huh?"

"Are you planning to be a London tour guide all your life? Is this the peak of your ambitions?"

He wrinkled his nose. "I haven't decided what I want to be. I was doing an Art History degree, but... yeah. Let's not talk about that. Let's just say I like my art. I'm gonna paint a new placard for those protestor women, you know, get some of my art out there, but..." He sighed.

"What's up?"

"I tell you one thing I don't like about London. How easy it is to be invisible here."

Diana wanted to tell him that was one of the perks of the city, the easy anonymity for those who sought it. But she sensed that wasn't what he was getting at.

"I've been doing my sketches," he said, "working with my paints and posting it all online. And sure, there's some likes, but you know what my most-liked photo of the past week is?"

He swiped on his phone for a few seconds, and then held it out to her.

It was a picture of Zaf on the stairs leading from Westminster Hall, his face pressed up to that of an ugly brass dragon statue, pulling an equally ugly face.

"And that's only because it got boosted by a bunch of students," he said.

"It's a good photo," she said, then frowned as she caught a detail in the background.

Diana reached out. She pinched her fingers to zoom in on the image.

As she did so, it sparked a memory of the combination of scents she associated with the Palace of Westminster.

"Well, I never," she said.

## Chapter Thirty-Five

"What is it?" asked Zaf.

"Just thinking of what passes unnoticed in the background." Diana returned his phone to him. "Invisible, like you say. Can you forward that to me?"

"Er, sure," said Zaf, wondering what she was on about. "Point is that if you're trying to get noticed as a creative, it's tough."

"You have an eye for the beautiful, Zaf. You are, if I may say, a very stylish young man."

Zaf tugged at the T-shirt he'd thrown on after his shower.

She nodded. "I have a feeling you might be interested in a little job I have to do. Bryan upstairs died recently, and I need to take a look round and remove any clothing I don't want to leave for the contract cleaners."

Zaf wrinkled his nose. "You want me to help you clear out a dead guy's clothes? I'm not sure—"

"You might be surprised. Bryan mixed with all sorts of creatives. There could be treasure up there."

Zaf licked a crumb of cake off his thumb. "OK. Let's

explore this Aladdin's cave, then." He stood up. "If there's vintage fashion to be uncovered then I have the nose of a bloodhound. Or a clotheshound."

"I'm pretty sure that there's no such thing," said Diana. "But let's see what your nose is like."

Zaf couldn't quite believe the size of these flats. Each one was a single floor in what would have been an enormous house, but even a single floor was a lot bigger than anywhere he'd ever lived. Bryan's flat was on the top floor, so the ceilings were lower and the windows not as vast as Diana's. But it was still massive.

"So what did Bryan do when he was alive?" he asked as they walked through the living room. A film of dust coated the surfaces and objects, many of which were musical instruments that looked like distant relatives of the ones Zaf was used to. A funny-looking wooden guitar thing that might have been a mandolin sat on a shelf beside some sort of tiny metal harp.

"He was a session musician," Diana said. "Multi-instrumental. Talented. Guitars, drums, woodwind, you name it. He was in great demand throughout his career. If you flick through his vinyl collection, I guarantee he'll have played on most of the albums."

"You knew him a long time then?"

Diana nodded. "We both came here around the same time, in the early eighties. He wasn't always home, he was away on tours for months at a time."

"So did he play all of these things?" Zaf pointed at the collection of dusty instruments.

"He could get a tune or a rhythm out of any instrument. Sometimes he'd come back with something he'd found at a flea market and tinker with it until either he could play it, or he'd decided it was really just an ornament."

She looked around, her face sad. "Many of the instruments have gone now. The really special ones were named in his will and left to friends or people he admired."

There was a large space in the room. Zaf walked over to it, eyeing the dents in the carpet "Hang on. Was there a grand piano in here?"

"There was."

"Wow."

"Come on, it's the wardrobe we're here to see." Diana headed out of the room.

Zaf followed her through to where he'd been expecting to find a bedroom. But there was no bed, just clothes rails and some cupboard storage, with shoe racks lined up underneath the rails.

"Is this whole room a wardrobe?" he asked.

Diana nodded. "Walk-in wardrobe, dressing room, not sure what the correct term is. See anything that takes your fancy?"

Zaf stopped admiring the room and focused on the clothes. There were more of them than in a shop. There was even a rail dedicated to hats, each one hanging from a little clip.

"I've never been a hat person," he said, "but I could be." He picked up a yellow hat with a brim and put it on his head. He bobbed in front of the mirror and grinned at himself. "Is this a fedora?"

"It looks rather good on you," Diana said. "Makes me think of Jimi Hendrix."

"Who?"

She widened her eyes

Zaf grinned and struck an air guitar pose. "Jimi. I know."

Diana shook her head, moving along the hooks. "There's one in red, too."

Diana moved away to flick through a row of jackets, while Zaf tried on more hats.

"I don't know. Does a proper hat say I'm a grown-up? I look at me wearing these and I feel a bit fake."

"If a hat's not for you, then move on," she told him. "Plenty more items to look at."

"When you say we can take what we like, does that really mean as much as we want?"

"It does. Nothing good will happen to whatever stays here." She gave him a wink. "Fill your boots."

Zaf flicked through some shirts. He checked the size: they'd fit. He pulled out a floral shirt in oranges and browns.

"Oh, bruv. The colours on this!"

He put it over his arm and carried on flicking through, but as he pulled out more and more, he realised his arm was starting to ache. He found a chair to drape his finds over.

He looked over to see what Diana was doing. "Have you found anything?"

"There's a nice collection of scarves. If we're to be subjected to horrible corporate fleeces then I'll need a pop of colour at the neckline." She stood at the mirror and held them against her face.

"And everywhere else you can put one." Zaf joined her at the mirror. He draped each of his ears with a scarf then wrapped one around his head. He pouted. "Do I look like the Karate Kid?"

"Not sure about that. Maybe like a young Carl Douglas."

"Who?"

"The *Kung Fu Fighting* guy. I met him once at Biddu Appaiah's recording studios. I was very *very* young."

"You act like you know everyone in London, Diana."

"Maybe I do." She laughed. "Hey, how d'you feel about corduroy?"

Zaf saw where she was pointing. "I love a bit of corduroy. Do I spy velvet as well?"

He picked out a corduroy overshirt and a velvet jacket. He pulled the velvet jacket on over his t-shirt and checked himself in the mirror. It was a deep blue colour and its pile gave it a sleek sheen that caught the light as he moved.

"This will look amazing on the dance floor."

Diana was still leafing through clothes. "How about some houndstooth check?"

"I don't even know what that is."

"Classic weave design." She held up a hanger. "It's a quality wool jacket by the looks of things. The brown and tan colours are unusual."

"I like it." Zaf couldn't quite believe his luck: all these fantastic clothes for free. "Where did Bryan get all this stuff from? There's not even labels in most of it."

"The way I understand it," Diana replied, "up-and-coming fashion students would often make a gift of their designs to successful musicians. It was a way of getting their stuff out there. A bit like influencers now. I doubt they were all given directly to Bryan, but he was a bit of a magpie." She straightened. "I'm going to check out his belts and bags. Want me to find a holdall or a case to hold your haul?"

He hesitated "If I pack this stuff all neat and tidy in a case, d'you reckon I'd be able to leave it somewhere for a few days?"

"I'd have thought so." Diana gave a small gasp. "Good grief, there's a Hussar's jacket over there."

She held up a fancy old-fashioned military jacket in dark wool with gold braiding in horizontal stripes. "Back in the eighties, Adam Ant wore something like this and everyone wanted one. Including me." She shrugged it on and looked in the mirror. "Hm, a bit overblown now, but it is magnificent."

"Overblown should be my middle name." Zaf removed the velvet jacket and held out a hand for the military jacket. He shrugged it on and puffed out his chest. "I already feel important. The gold braid's going straight to my head."

"It's too formal like that. You need to hang it casually, in a pirate style."

"Arrr."

Diana folded her arms across her chest, surveying him. "You'd have loved the early eighties. Go back through the shirts and find something with ruffles."

"What's the chance of me finding an eye patch?" he asked.

Diana gave a shrug and gestured around the room. "With Bryan, I wouldn't be surprised. A cutlass and a parrot too, maybe?"

Zaf whirled round, his arms outstretched. "This is crazy. How could a session musician afford to rent such a huge place in London?"

"We were lucky," Diana said. "London wasn't always like this. Back in the eighties, there were a lot of run-down properties. Empty houses. Canary Wharf was still just derelict wasteland. Bryan and I got these places on a deal that I guess you'd call a peppercorn rent contract."

"Peppercorn?"

"We paid a modest fee to live in and look after the flats, and the contract was so badly worded that as long as we remained the sitting tenants, that rent would never change."

"You got these places dirt cheap."

"And will continue to." Her shoulders sagged. "Or at least, I will. Alexsei, my landlord, he can rent this out for whatever he likes now Bryan has gone."

Zaf moved to the window. Evening was settling over the city but the square was still visible in the grey.

"Are all these houses like this, full of old tenants?"

"Less of the old, young man."

He laughed. "*Long-term* tenants with cheap rents."

Diana gave a huff of laughter. "Most of these houses are empty again. Well over half."

"What?"

"London property's so expensive. People buy it as an investment, like gold and diamonds. A lot of foreign investors."

"Russian oligarchs."

"Alexsei's dad, Mr Dadashov, who really owns this house, is Azerbaijani. But, yes, wealthy businesspeople have bought up these places with no real intention of living in them or letting other people live in them."

Zaf cast off the extravagant jacket in annoyance. "That's ridiculous."

"That's one way of looking at it."

He spun round to look at her, anger on his face. "You don't get it. They expect me to work in central London but it costs all my monthly salary to rent a single room anywhere near here. I saw somewhere for seven hundred a month the other day, I thought my luck was in. And then I looked closer and realised it was just a parking space on a driveway. Seven hundred a month for a parking space! How am I supposed to compete in such a stupid system?"

Diana gave him a sad smile. "Chapman-Moore's homeless bill should try to address some of that."

He snorted.

"You know," she said. "We could take a look at the Fairview New Start building."

"We could?"

She raised an eyebrow. "A seemingly benign government policy to provide housing for those that need it. But *we* know something isn't quite right."

"So, we just go take a look?" Zaf said.

"Why not? Grab your coat." Diana gestured about. "Grab any coat."

## Chapter Thirty-Six

It was a forty-minute journey across London, a simple trip along the District Line from Victoria to Bow Road station. In Victoria, Diana's eyes were drawn towards the information boards, but instead of forlorn lovers there was just the usual assortment of travelling tourists.

They walked up the wide expanse of Bow Street.

"My mum lives half a mile that way," Diana said. "Got herself a little flat."

"Wow," said Zaf.

Diana eyed him suspiciously. "Was that *gosh, I can't believe your mum is still alive, Diana?*"

"No. It was a, er, *wow, what a lovely area for her to live in.*"

"Hmmm. Nice save."

"Never tempted to have her come and live with you?"

"Oh, she's an old school Eastender. I think she believes that if she ever left the area she'd crumble into dust like a vampire."

"You don't sound like an Eastender."

"Oh, you mean I don't sound like a proper Cockney? What d'you want? A Dick van Dyke impression? Here."

*Here* was the turning into Fairfield Road, and somewhere up there was John Chapman-Moore's property development.

Short leafy trees lined a road of square brown-brick buildings. London's East End had seen decades of gentrification, but it still had a very different character from Diana's square in Pimlico.

"Just up the road from here is the site of the match girls' strike in the late nineteenth century," Diana said as they walked.

"That sounds like the punch line to a Christmas cracker joke."

"It was a landmark piece of industrial action. The girls and women worked in hazardous and gruelling conditions. They went on strike, and managed to get some changes implemented."

"Good for them," said Zaf.

As they passed the large Stagecoach bus station, Zaf said, "I've just remembered. If Paul Kensington calls, there's a gas leak at the bus garage."

"Good grief. What's happened?"

"There isn't really, but Newton was worried the cat thing would freak Paul out. Now the lie might have got out of hand. We need to stick to the story that it's a propane tank from a few doors down that has breached."

Diana looked at Zaf. "Is Newton out of his depth?"

"Yeah, definitely."

"What I meant is, does he need help?"

"When I left, he was almost done with creating the cat dossier. It's like a work of art, you should see it. Anyway, he says the next step is some serious research into missing cats. He made it sound like geeky internet stuff. He's in his element."

They came to a stop at the address on the brochure.

"Hmmm. Is it me," said Zaf, "or is this building definitely not big enough to house – how many people was it?"

They peered up at a frontage that looked like a disused carpet shop with a flat above it. Diana checked the sheet in her hand.

"Single-living accommodation for two hundred people."

"That's just plain wrong."

"Let's give it the benefit of the doubt for a moment," said Diana. "Maybe it's a tiny frontage with a huge building somewhere behind?"

"Bit of a TARDIS. Like ten Downing Street."

"Exactly."

"It should be easy to check that out." Zaf pointed to a narrow alley running up the side. In the dark, they used their phones as torches. Diana's shoulders rubbed against grubby brickwork as they followed the alley through to a narrow thoroughfare behind the Fairview New Start building and its neighbouring properties. They walked along, behind the carpet shop. There was a small fenced-off area. Zaf reached over and unlatched the gates, and they went inside.

Nothing but bins.

The back wall had a small window of frosted glass, a bathroom, perhaps. Zaf cocked his head. "Big door."

"Easier to roll carpets out of," Diana said.

She tried the door, but it was locked. She pushed on the frosted window, which shifted a little.

"Are we actually doing this?" whispered Zaf.

"You don't want to?"

Zaf gave a small shrug: *why not?* The window opened outwards, so Diana dug her fingers under the edge and pulled. It opened on very creaky hinges.

"It's not latched," she hissed as she pulled it wide and peered inside a toilet cubicle.

"You're not thinking about climbing in there?" Zaf's eyes were wide.

"I'm committed to finding out the truth about this place. How about you?"

"It feels properly fishy, but are you expecting me to wriggle through there into some ancient loo?"

Diana looked him up and down. She'd thought Zaf might be more gung-ho than this.

She clenched her jaw. "I might need you to give me a leg up, or perhaps I can stand on a bin."

There was an old-style metal dustbin with a lid. They managed to carry it over in complete silence, using the handles on either side.

"I'd do the decent thing and go up myself, but I don't think I'd fit through that window," Zaf said.

"With luck I can let you in once I'm inside. Now, hold this bin steady, will you?"

## Chapter Thirty-Seven

Diana held Zaf's shoulder as she hoisted herself up onto the bin. She straightened and then moved across to the window, swinging a leg inside the aperture to straddle the sill. She kicked the toilet seat down with her toe then slid across so she was standing on top of the toilet.

"I'm in. See you in a moment."

She flicked on her phone torch and left the cubicle and then the bathroom, turning right towards where she imagined the back door would be. She was relieved to see a key in the lock.

She opened the door and let Zaf inside. "Welcome."

Zaf slid inside and closed the door. They stared down the corridor.

"What if someone's living in the flat upstairs?" he whispered.

"Let's examine the ground floor, quiet as we can. Then we can work out what to do about upstairs."

They crept through into the shop, careful to shield their

lights. The place was empty of carpets but still held that carpet smell, along with dust and damp.

Diana went to the counter. On top of it lay scattered bits of paperwork, mostly carpet-fitting invoices. It looked like the place had still been trading until a year ago.

Diana and pointed at a winking red light in the upper corner of the room. "We've triggered an alarm."

"Nah. It's probably on standby mode." Zaf was looking around the space. "This place isn't all that big at all. The shop is the full width, and we walked the length down that alleyway. The flat upstairs'll be the same size. Unless they're planning to build ten storeys on top, I can't see how this can house that many people."

"You're right," said Diana. "Let's backtrack and check the back door."

They crept back down the corridor towards the back door.

"Did you hear something?" Zaf said.

"You're just spooked," Diana told him. "We just need to keep calm for a few more minutes."

"I definitely heard someth—"

Diana stopped: she'd heard it too.

In the light of her torch, she spotted the back door handle moving.

"In here!" she hissed.

They both scuttled into the bathroom and shut themselves inside the toilet cubicle. It was a tight squeeze. They stood stock still, their torches off, hardly daring to breathe.

Diana heard the back door open and someone stepping inside. Zaf had hold of her sleeve, his grip registering every sound.

There was the heavy sound of the key being turned in the lock, and the clatter as it was removed.

Diana felt Zaf's hand on her arm: he'd heard it. He knew what it meant, too.

A voice called out. "Right, you little scrotes! I know you're in here!"

Zaf held up his light so Diana could see his lips mouth, "*What do we do?*"

Wide-eyed, she mouthed back, "*I don't know.*"

"I *will* find you," called the gruff voice. It was a proper East End voice, a fighting-in-pub-car-parks voice. "You might as well come out now. I ain't called the old bill. We don't call the old bill."

Zaf mouthed, "*Should we call the police?*"

Diana frowned, trying to focus on the voice.

"I can be a reasonable man," said the voice, making it clear the reasonableness was only a possibility, "but I warn you that my patience is on a knife edge now you've disturbed my evening."

Diana reached for the door lock.

"What are you doing?" Zaf hissed at her side.

She eased open the door and stepped into the corridor. She couldn't see the man fully beyond the glare of his light.

"Ah, there you are," the man leered.

"Chaz? Chaz Chase?" she said.

The man hesitated. "Miss Bakewell. Is that you?"

"It is, Chaz."

The man sighed deeply. "Oh, missus, you are in a lot of trouble."

## Chapter Thirty-Eight

Two minutes later, Zaf and Diana had been bundled into the back of a black London cab and were being driven off. Where to, Zaf had no idea.

Although Diana apparently knew this shaven-headed East End thug in a tweed jacket, Zaf didn't get the impression that they were entirely out of the woods. He knew that one of the key features of a London cab was the unbreakable window between the driver and the large passenger area, and that another feature was that the driver controlled all the door locks.

"Where are we going?" he asked.

"Auntie Lipman's," said the driver, who he'd heard Diana call Chaz.

Zaf mouthed at Diana. "Who's Auntie Lipman?"

"Auntie Lipman's is a caff, Zaf," said Chaz with a faint smile. "Opens late and serves the sort of food you need if you're not gonna see your bed for a while."

Zaf didn't like the suggestion they weren't going to see their beds for a while.

Twenty or so minutes later they arrived at a brightly-lit café, open despite the late hour, with red and white plastic tablecloths and a vintage menu printed on a vinyl banner above the counter. It was empty apart from the aproned woman behind the counter and a bullet-headed man with greying temples sitting at one of the tables. The man shifted his rounded shoulders and eyed the arrivals with obvious amusement.

"Diana Bakewell, well I never. If I was to list all the people I thought I might find breaking and entering into one of my buildings, I've got to say you wouldn't have made the top five hundred."

"Hello, Ernie." Her tone was friendly, but Zaf noticed she didn't take a step towards him.

The man rose from his seat. "Not got a hug for your Uncle Ernie?"

Diana strode towards him, no hesitation now. They wrapped their arms around each other.

"He's your uncle?" asked Zaf.

"I'm everyone's uncle, sunshine," replied the man.

Diana gestured awkwardly at herself and Zaf. "Ernie, this looks bad, I realise that. We're going to explain what we were doing, because in reality it's very reasonable."

"Is it, though?" Zaf said.

Ernie looked Zaf up and down. "Son, if Diana says she's got reasons then I'm all ears."

"This here is Zaf. Zaf, meet Big Ernie," said Diana.

"Big Ernie?"

The man was a little above average height and maybe a fraction overweight.

Ernie patted his stomach. "Went to Weight Watchers after

the last scare. Lost eight stone. Names stick longer than love handles." He pointed at the counter. "Beryl's doing me a Monty in the Hole. You want something?"

The prices on the board were written in marker pen, and Zaf could see the shadow of whatever the old prices had been.

"I haven't had a fish finger sandwich for years," he said. "If I can put tomato sauce all over it, I might just revert to being ten years old."

"A mushroom omelette for me," said Diana.

Ernie gave a nod. "You 'ear that, Beryl? Add it to the order. And one of them fancy coffees for Chaz."

Ernie's man, Chaz, had taken a seat by himself at the table nearest the door. Zaf realised he was guarding the door, to stop people entering. Or leaving.

Ernie, Diana and Zaf sat at a table beneath a chipped cork noticeboard full of small ads on postcards. Beryl came over with a huge brown teapot and set it down on the table.

She returned with Ernie's order: a full English breakfast stuffed into a giant Yorkshire pudding. Ernie spotted the look on Zaf's face.

"You've heard of a full monty?"

"I've heard of *The* Full Monty."

"And you've heard of a toad in the hole. Well, this is a Monty in the Hole."

"Don't you go spreading that idea around, Ernie," said Beryl. "There's only you that can get away with taking liberties with our menu like that."

Ernie gave them all an expansive shrug. "They know they could make a killing if they put it on the regular menu, but they like to keep it our little secret."

Diana poured them all a cup of tea from the chunky pot. "So, Ernie, we owe you an explanation."

"You do." Ernie pushed sausage and eggs onto his fork.

"First of all, I had no idea the building was one of yours. We were under the impression that it belongs to John Chapman-Moore, the MP."

"He rents it off me, so you're half right," said Ernie. "You know me, though, I protect my assets, so I have the sort of alarm system that isn't obvious to the casual thief. People soon learn to leave my places alone when they have the right sort of education."

Zaf looked across at Diana. This man, Ernie, was talking like an East End crime boss. Zaf thought people like that only existed in Guy Ritchie films. Diana seemed very familiar with him, which to Zaf was almost as chilling.

He decided to keep a low profile. Diana's expression was giving nothing away. He sighed and turned his attention to the adverts pinned to the noticeboard on the wall next to them.

"So, Chapman-Moore, does he have plans to rebuild the place, then?" asked Diana. "It's a great spot, but the proposal he's putting forward to the government is that he'll house two hundred homeless people in there."

Diana filled Ernie in on the events of the last few days, and the documents that Florence had been collecting.

Ernie chuckled. "I think you've correctly identified what we might call a *dodgy deal* there, Diana. I wish I could tell you how rare they are, because people are honourable, but of course I'd be lying."

Diana leaned back in her chair and scowled at Ernie. "I'm not an idiot, Ernie. But I assumed the government would check up on things like an *entire actual building*."

"You might think that, but there are plenty of other examples. Remember when the government gave a multi-million-pound ferry contract to a company with no ferries?"

"No!" said Zaf. "Did that really happen?"
Ernie and Diana both nodded.
"The world's crazy," said Zaf.
They both nodded again.

# Chapter Thirty-Nine

"So what's your story, Zaf?" asked Ernie, digging deeper into his massive meal. "You're not a local, are you?"

"I'm from Birmingham," said Zaf.

"And how are you liking it in London?"

"I really like it here, it's got loads going for it, but the cost of living is stupidly high." He stabbed a finger at a yellow card pinned to the wall. "Look at this here. Room for rent. It's one of the cheapest rooms in this listing and they want eight hundred pounds a month."

"That's about the going rate," said Ernie.

"Ha! *Wanted, quiet type to share small clean flat with young professional.* So you pay all that money for a room and you're going around on tiptoes the whole time? It's ridiculous."

The word *quiet* was highlighted with little flower-like asterisks.

"Ridiculous is the word," Ernie agreed.

Beryl turned up with the fish finger sandwich and the omelette. The service here was obscenely quick, but the food looked good.

"So how do you know Diana?" asked Ernie.

"We work together." Zaf bit into the sandwich. It was superb, in the way that only comfort food at inappropriate mealtimes could be.

"You still at Chartwell and Crouch?" Ernie asked Diana. "At least you'll have seen off that weasel Paul Kensington by now, surely?"

"He's very much still in charge." Diana pulled a face.

"What? So does that mean Morris is still inside?" Ernie asked.

Zaf had never heard the name Morris. "Morris who?"

"Morris Walker. Yes, he was found guilty on all counts," said Diana.

"Summat wrong there." Ernie shook his head. "I should've had a word, got him a better brief, y'know?"

"It's done now," Diana said. "It just worries me that Paul Kensington will destroy the whole character of the company in the meantime. Some of his ideas are hideous."

"Corporate arse-lickers, 'scuse my French. They're the same the world over."

They all ate in silence for a few moments.

"So, who is Morris Walker?" asked Zaf. "Was he the boss before Paul Kensington?"

Diana nodded but said no more.

Zaf ate the last of his sandwich. He was tempted to have another, but knew he'd regret it. Ernie had somehow made his teetering Jenga tower of breakfast mostly disappear in the same timeframe.

"Are we..." Diana flicked a finger between herself and Ernie. "Are we OK?"

Ernie's face darkened, for just a second.

"Always lovely to catch up with an old mate, Diana," he said, "but next time you could just give me a bell, eh?"

"Of course," she said.

"Chaz here will drive you home," said Ernie.

"Oh, we couldn't impose," replied Diana.

The darkness in Ernie's face returned for a second. "I insist."

Zaf saw the brittleness in Diana's smile.

Zaf and Diana stepped outside, and found Chaz immediately behind them.

"This way," he said, gesturing to his cab.

"Hang on," said Diana and crossed the road.

"I'm taking you home, luv," said Chaz.

"In a minute," said Diana.

She stood outside the window of a stationer's shop and peered in at the display window. Zaf joined her, looking through the glass.

"Thinking of taking up watercolours?" he suggested.

"Vegan paint," said Diana, pointing. "Environmentally-friendly paper. Vegan bamboo pens. Cruelty-free dyes."

"Yes?" said Zaf.

Diana looked at the café. "Bethnal Green. Little flowers." She pursed her lips. "It almost all makes sense."

"What does?" he said. It was late. She would be tired: how old was Diana, anyway? "It sounds like you're having an episode."

She scowled at him. "Come on. Best not keep Chaz waiting."

They returned to the cab and Chaz drove them in silence back to Eccleston Square. He didn't ask for an address.

As Chaz disappeared into the night, Zaf watched the red taillights of the taxi.

"Your friend, Ernie..." he said.

"Yes?"

"Is he, you know, a bit dodgy or something?"

Diana laughed. "A bit dodgy? No, he's definitely a *lot* dodgy. Things were a bit touch and go there."

"Really? I thought he was your uncle. I thought you were friends."

"No, he's not my uncle. Yes, he is my friend. But Ernie isn't so sentimental that he won't break a friend's arm if they've stepped over the line."

"You're kidding."

Diana gave him a look.

"He's got a finger in a lot of different pies," she said, "and I'm not sure I want to know about most of them. There's one thing I'm fairly sure about though."

"Oh?"

"At heart, he's a good guy. In the broader scheme of things. He is a good person who might do a few slightly less-good things."

Zaf thought about that. "Yeah. Aren't we all a bit like that?"

## Chapter Forty

Despite not needing to resume tour guide duties until the afternoon, Diana woke early on Thursday. Her mind turned over the events of the past few days.

She had no idea how the police investigation into Florence's death was going but she felt, rather than thought, that she could almost see the shape of who had killed Florence and why. There were just a few questions left.

She padded about her flat, wearing her vintage kimono while she sipped her morning tea. She settled into a chair near the large window overlooking the garden in the square, interested to see which birds were squabbling over the feeders, and whether any new flowers had bloomed overnight.

What she hadn't expected to see was Zaf closing the door of the shed behind him. He shouldered his duffle bag and walked to a well-covered part of the fence before heaving himself over the railings.

"Oh, Zaf."

She sighed, disappointed with herself for not acting on the signs. He had split with his boyfriend and had nowhere to live.

He'd spent at least one night simply partying, but that must have caught up with him by now. He was homeless and had decided that the relative safety of the shed in the garden square was his best bet.

She couldn't fault his logic. No wonder he'd wanted to leave the case full of clothes in Bryan's flat. He was searching for something he could afford on his wages from Chartwell and Crouch, which would be a tall order indeed.

She considered rushing down to intercept him, but decided that wasn't the wisest idea. She'd find a subtler way to talk to him about it.

But before she went to work, she had a little matter to check.

She got out her phone, looked up the name of the art supply shop in Bethnal Green, and phoned them.

"Yes, hello," she said when they picked up. "I wonder if you could help me with a question about an item that you stock…"

## Chapter Forty-One

When Zaf arrived, still yawning, at the bus depot he heard a distant mewling. Was one of the cats in trouble?

He rushed over to the corner near the office to see where it was coming from. He didn't like leaving an animal in distress.

But it wasn't a cat.

"Newton?" Zaf called as he entered the kitchen. He could see Newton's legs sticking out, but the driver's top half was invisible, covered by a writhing mountain of cats.

If the number of cats had been impressive while they were spread all around the garage, it was downright terrifying when they were all piled on top of Zaf's colleague.

"Newton!" He pulled on Newton's legs to drag him away but the cats came too, scuffling and skidding to maintain whatever position they had.

"What are you all doing, you daft moggies?"

He started from the top and removed a cat. It spat at him and ran away to a corner.

"What's going on, Newton? Are you alive in there? What have they done to you?"

Newton flung an arm out to the side. A small furry tidal wave followed the movement. Whatever the cats wanted, it was in Newton's hand. His face was exposed now, although his arm was crushed by the squirming mass.

"I didn't think this through," he said. "I got a tub of catnip as a treat. Now they won't let me put the lid on."

"Where is the lid?" Zaf looked around and spotted it on the floor at Newton's feet. "Here, let me help."

He removed another cat from the mêlée, then realised it was the same one he had moved previously. It had just run around and rejoined the fun.

"*Pspsps*," tried Zaf, but the cat noise had no power against the feline desire for catnip.

"How about I help you to your feet?" Zaf suggested.

He held onto Newton's other arm and pulled him up. If he'd expected the cats to fall away in one giant cat avalanche, he was disappointed. It was as if Newton was a cat magnet. Cats swung on his arm like a huge furry pendulum.

"How are they doing that?"

"With their claws," said Newton, through gritted teeth. "And their teeth."

Zaf went to Newton's tool bench, found a pair of leather work gloves, and put them on. He returned, took a breath, and plunged his hands into the writhing mass, reaching down for the tub. He pried cats away, dropping them to the floor and ignoring Newton's howls of pain. Eventually he got down to the last cat.

"Oh," said Newton, "that's the evil one that seems fond of chewing gloves, so you should watch ou—"

As Zaf tugged, the cat disengaged from the catnip. It

turned and sank its teeth into Zaf's gloved hand. The thick leather blunted the sharpness of its teeth, but its jaw clamped down hard on Zaf's fingers, so now he was the one supporting a cat hanging in mid-air.

"Ow! My god, this thing is a monster!" shouted Zaf.

The tan and black cat stared up at him as it swung on the end of his arm. There was no regret in its gaze, only malice.

Zaf managed to pull his hand out of the glove as he lowered the cat to the floor. It ran off with the glove in its mouth.

"We should get the lid on that catnip," he said. "And we should definitely get some ointment on your arm."

Newton nodded, blinking. Blood ran down his forearms, but he seemed oblivious to his scratches.

"Did you see the mind map?" Newton asked, nodding to the wall outside.

"No, mate. I was distracted by you being the base of a cat mountain."

Diana entered the kitchen with the sleek grey tabby Newton had christened Gus in her arms. She had the open tub of catnip in her other hand.

"I met this handsome fellow trying to drag this tin away across the depot floor. I'm assuming you didn't give it to him."

Gus made a playful but half-hearted swipe at Diana's hand.

"Gus, you sneaky thief," said Newton. He took the tub from her, put the lid back on and placed it in a top cupboard before removing the cat from her arms.

Diana picked cat hairs off her blazer. Zaf fetched the green plastic first aid box for Newton's cuts and went to put the kettle on.

"Best clean those scratches," Zaf said.

"I'm not sure why you brought catnip into the depot," said Diana. "We're trying to encourage them to leave, not to stay."

"They're here now," said Newton. "I thought they could do with some entertaining."

"Let's put our energies into getting rid of them, not making them welcome. Next thing, you'll be building a giant version of one of those cat playhouses with the scratching posts and what have you."

"I won't," said Newton, sounding very much as if he was halfway through doing that exact thing.

He took Gus out into the depot proper to join the other cats while Zaf put teabags into the teapot.

"Sleep well last night?" said Diana lightly.

Zaf had his back to her a good thing, or she might have seen his look of guilty surprise. The truth was, in the shed in her garden square he'd slept better than he had in weeks.

"Why do you ask?" he said, as casually as he could.

"I guess it's been an emotionally difficult week, what with your split from Malachi and that. And we got picked up by my... unusual uncle Ernie. Which unnerves some people. I was just checking."

"Ah, I see." He poured hot water into the pot. "Yes. Very rested."

He put the teapot on the table and got out cups. They weren't collecting the school group until the afternoon.

Diana glanced over her shoulder at the door to the depot. She could hear Newton talking to the cats. Perhaps explaining why they couldn't have the promised cat treehouse.

"The cats absolutely mobbed Newton before you got here," said Zaf. "A right pile-on."

"Surprisingly, the man is an emotional pushover," said Diana. "I suspect his children run him ragged."

Zaf shrugged. "But while Newton was fending off all the cats, Gus was simply dragging away the catnip unnoticed, almost like he'd planned it that way."

"You think that was his plan all along?" Diana sniffed the milk for freshness and helped pour the teas. "Distractions," she said Diana. "The death of Florence Breecher. The murderer only succeeded because everyone was distracted."

"Yes."

"Without the protestor, Catalina Arenosa, the killer's efforts would have been seen immediately. But how would you know that was going to happen? That cat, Gus, is an opportunist thief. I'm not sure our murderer was so casual or so lucky."

Zaf nodded in agreement. He sipped his tea. It was hot and felt cleansing. Several nights of sleeping rough had left him feeling grubby and unlovable. He didn't know how much longer he could continue like this.

"Of course," he said, "it's also a bit like what happened in John Chapman-Moore's office."

"How so?"

"With all the students squashed in... like catnip-addicted cats if you like—"

"I don't think I could describe them as addicted to politics *or* John Chapman Moore MP."

"OK, but squashed in there, being entertained, everyone was so packed so close together that the murderer could have stolen the letter opener without others seeing." He slurped his tea. "I guess that sometimes there being lots of people about is as useful as there being none."

# Chapter Forty-Two

With the morning to himself, Zaf wondered if he had time to do some work on the Fat Cat placard he had planned. After his morning cuppa, he went out into the main depot.

"Newton mate, I don't suppose there's any stiff card or board around here?"

"Have a look over there," said Newton, pointing to a dark corner. "Good luck rescuing it from the cats, though."

Zaf rummaged around. There were a lot of cardboard boxes here that he'd not noticed before. Maybe Newton had something in mind. He found a suitable piece of board to paint on. When he turned it over, he realised that it was an old price list for ice creams. Nothing on the list cost more than 50p.

"I bet this is an actual antique," he called out to Newton, but got no response. Newton was on the phone to a potential cat owner.

Which cat to use as a model, though?

Zaf's gaze came to rest on Gus. The cat sat on the table, his eyes level with Zaf's.

"What?" Zaf said to the cat. "Are you trying to tell me you want me to paint you?" He looked the cat up and down. "You're too nice-looking. I need a fat cat. I need a model that looks meaner."

As if summoned by his words, the tan and black cat appeared. It jumped up on the table near to Gus and swiped at him with a paw as it passed. Gus didn't react.

"Now you *do* look pretty mean, it's true," Zaf told the newcomer. "'I'm sure your mother loved you, but you're not the nicest cat I've ever met. Can you sit still while I paint you?"

He considered: did cats' mothers love them? He wondered where this lot had all come from, if there were families somewhere pining.

The tan and black cat positioned itself in front of Gus in what looked like a deliberate attempt to usurp his position. It sat there, motionless, as if it understood what Zaf wanted from it.

Zaf painted as quickly as he could, trying to capture the cat's expression. The darkness of its eyes glittered with intelligence, but there was no hint of cuteness there. It had black lines around its eyes, like a drag queen who'd been a little heavy-handed with the eyeliner. Even its whiskers arched upwards in a flick of arrogance. The angle of its head and the small twitch of its tail all spoke of a cat that had some serious napping or killing to do.

"I bet you're well camouflaged when it's dark," said Zaf, not sure why he was making conversation with the cat. It seemed polite, given the creature was sitting for a portrait. "We won't take much longer now. I think I've captured your essence."

He stood back, surveying his work. He had the general feel

of its face and its basic shape. "You do make a very good fat cat," he told it.

It wasn't that the cat was plump, but its malevolence was just right for on Zaf's portrait. He added the wording FAT CATS OUT! as Newton appeared beside him.

"That's a very good picture," Newton said.

"It's like he wanted me to paint him."

"She," Newton corrected.

"Right. I had no idea."

"We've got no leads on the owner for this one," Newton said. "I think we've got possibilities for nearly all of the cats now, but this one and Gus are in the Billy-No-Mates club."

"Aww." Zaf reached out a hand to fuss the tan and black cat. "Does she have a name?"

Before Newton could answer, the cat had dug its claws deep into Zaf's outstretched hand. As she pinned it to the table, she leaned her head down and casually bit into his knuckle. Not deep enough to break the skin, but deep enough to send a firm message.

Zaf snatched his hand back. "Ow! This one's evil. You bad cat."

"A name, you say?" Newton mused, as if he hadn't even witnessed the attack. "She's a warrior, for sure. I wondered if she could be Boudicca."

"Are cats called Boudicca?" Zaf asked, nursing his hand.

"Yeah, I think so." Newton turned away.

Boudicca it was, then.

# Chapter Forty-Three

Diana popped out of the depot and returned fifteen minutes later with bacon and sausage rolls from the *Tasty for You* café.

Zaf's stomach rumbled as the scent of the hot sandwiches reached his nostrils.

"You're a life saver, Diana," he said. "Any idea if Paul Kensington's gonna stay away today?" He turned to survey the depot and the many cats. "If he comes in now, we're in real trouble."

"I can see that," said Diana. "You're sure Newton's making progress?"

As he devoured his sandwich, Zaf showed her the crazy wall of cat pictures and potential owners, with the lines of string linking it all together.

"You know, it's in our interest to help him with the rehoming," said Zaf. "I think he's enjoying having these cats to stay. Did you see what he built for them?"

Zaf led Diana to a corner where a pile of cardboard boxes had been reconfigured into an eccentric adventure playground for cats. There were platforms and interconnected rooms with little windows and doors, at multiple levels.

"He got a load of those cardboard tubes from somewhere. I am pretty sure a cat can go in at one end and come out at the other without seeing the light of day."

"This is remarkable," said Diana."

"It's pretty bonkers, yeah."

"No, I mean look at the way they are using it," said Diana, pointing. "Most of the cats are sitting in that open box on the floor over there. They are all jockeying for position in that one place. And just one cat seems to have claimed the fancy treehouse all for itself. I can hear it stalking through the tunnels. Remind you of anything?"

"Wow. John Chapman-Moore's property development for the homeless," said Zaf. "Not open to the intended residents."

At that moment, the tan and black cat emerged at the very top of the tree and sat out on the little platform where the topmost boxes were fastened to a girder. She looked very pleased with herself as she washed her luxurious whiskers.

"It's Boudicca," said Zaf, pointing. "She is the actual poster girl for fat cats. I'd say she's very much underlining your point."

They walked back into the kitchen to find Newton.

"So, to be clear, have we managed to rehome a single cat yet?" Diana asked. "I can't even count how many there are altogether."

"It does look like a lot, but Newton's got appointments booked in all morning. I think he should move quite a few of them on."

Diana didn't look convinced, but Zaf kept the smile fixed on his face, as if he could resolve the cat crisis by force of will.

Diana was shocked by the sheer number of cats. "It's essential that we keep this from Paul Kensington."

Newton looked at her. "Well, yes. But how do we do that? Every time he phones, I can tell he's more suspicious."

She consulted her watch. "We don't have long."

"We do not."

"And a flimsy gas leak story won't do." Diana scooted a cat off one of the kitchen chairs with her umbrella and sat down. "Newton, I know I shouldn't ask this, but would you know anything about faking an email? I mean, making it look like it's come from someone else?"

"I do know something about that as it happens," said Newton. "I'm interested in such things. Not as a hacker, just because I'm curious."

Newton was someone Diana would describe as *professionally* curious.

"So," she asked, "would it be possible, in theory, to send Paul an email from his boss, asking him to check out a bus depot elsewhere, let's say in Leicester. Then we could send his boss an email from Paul, saying he's been invited to share best practices with a bus depot up in Leicester and that he was going to build up a possible business relationship, and..." She looked up at the driver.

Newton stared at her, incredulous. "So he goes up to Leicester for a day and just turns up at another bus depot?"

Diana shrugged. "Maybe we send another email to the Leicester bus depot, telling them he's some sort of expert and they can learn a lot from him if they show him round for the day. Wine and dine him, keep him overnight if at all possible."

Newton opened his laptop. "If it buys us the rest of today then maybe we can pull this off. Did you see I've started on the matching?"

While Newton was busy forging emails, Zaf walked Diana through the cat dossier on the wall.

"Mugshots and physical descriptions. It's quite the art installation," she said.

The cat dossier sprawled across several metres of wall. The lengths of string, labelled with questions and thoughts, linked missing cat posters with cats matching the descriptions. Printouts and notes covered the wall below the dossier. Some had photos from social media posts, while others just had notes. Newton had started some rudimentary matching.

"This is why it was clever to arrange the cat dossier by the type of cat," said Zaf. "So it's easier to match the available cats with the missing cats. I'm still not sure how he'll do it, though."

"It looks like a monumental task," Diana said.

"You think this is a monumental task?" Newton came up behind them. "Wait until I introduce you to the litter tray rota."

"Don't take this the wrong way," Zaf said, "but I always assumed you were a computer geek. Wouldn't this be easier if you put it in a spreadsheet or something?"

Newton shook his head. "I can't get all of the visual references onto a single screen. A picture paints a thousand words, Zaf."

"I can't help but think about the folder I was given," said Diana.

"What? The one from Florence's flat?" said Zaf and then pointed at the cat information on the wall. "These cat pictures. This reminded you of that folder."

She nodded. "It's like any communication." She looked pensive. "Any form of communication, whether it's a folder about property projects or a cat dossier or a protestor's placard, heck, even the music we sing in choir. Every form of communication carries more than one message."

"I had an Art professor who spoke like you."

"I'm sure you did. If someone came in now and saw this,

what would they think – apart from Newton being a madman?"

"That he wants to rehome cats."

"And?"

"He cares for cats?"

"And?"

"He has too much time on his hands?"

"Possibly," said Diana. "I think we're missing a trick with the folder. There's an extra meaning beyond that which we can already see. I see you've finished painting that fat cat sign you promised for the anti-poverty protestors."

"What d'you reckon?"

"It's good. I wondered if you'd mind letting me take it over to them?"

Zaf frowned. "You mean now? Why? We're going down there in a bit anyway, aren't we?"

"I need to ask them some questions."

Zaf's frown slipped into a slight smile. "Questions, eh? You turned detective, Diana?"

Diana straightened her back. "Tabitha Welkin entrusted me with a folder of information. The police seem uninterested in getting justice for the little people. I just want to put things right. Is there something wrong with that?"

Zaf's smile widened. "Nothing wrong at all. Go for it."

Diana nodded her thanks, picked up Zaf's placard, which was dry but still a little tacky, and stepped out onto the pavement.

# Chapter Forty-Four

Zaf returned his attention to the cat wall and, as an experiment, tried following the links that radiated out from a single missing cat poster. The missing cat was black, and it wasn't easy to tell if it also had some white patches. The dossier said it was a small, timid indoor cat and the string linked it to eight possible matches. Three of them were black cats, and the other five had small patches of white. As Zaf followed the string, he read the labels.

*This one is bold, match = 40%*
 *Timid but quite big, match = 50%*
 *Timid and small, match = 70%. Do lap test*

"What's the lap test?" he asked.

"I'm about to try it," said Newton, checking his watch. "Our first visitors of the day are arriving at any moment. Can you help me round up the candidates for the interview?"

"Eh?"

Newton prodded another of the missing cat posters on the wall. "These people here are coming. Follow the strings and you'll find the candidate cats they need to meet. We need to shut them all in Paul Kensington's office."

Zaf studied the poster. "So they've lost a black and white cat. We've got ten candidates. Ten?"

Newton shrugged. "There are lots of black and white cats and they didn't include a picture. Make sure you check which ones we want."

"Why don't I just grab every black and white cat I can catch and put them in the office?"

"Some are girls. This one is a boy," said Newton.

Zaf sighed. "I'm not all that good at telling the difference, Newton. How about I round up black and white cats galore and you can evict any you don't want when you've inspected them?"

"Fine. We can do it that way." Newton looked disappointed at such a cavalier approach.

Zaf still had one leather glove on. He tucked it into a pocket in case any of the cats turned out to be difficult.

Most of them were either lounging around or pacing curiously, so it wasn't hard to pick them up, although some wriggled and clawed in an attempt to get free. By the time he got to number three, Zaf had worked out that the back claws were the ones to look out for as the cats tried to spring from his arms.

He slid them one by one through a narrow gap in the door, using his spare hand and his legs to block the ones trying to escape.

"How many's that?" he called to Newton through the door.

"We need one more. I think it might be the one that keeps squeezing up the side of the fridge."

Zaf went to the kitchen to check. Sure enough, a black and white cat glared out from an impossibly narrow space between the fridge and the wall.

"Come on, then! *Pspsps!*"

The cat was unmoved. Zaf reached a hand in, but it shrank back. There was no obvious way to get hold of it in the tight space.

He went back to Newton. "How do I get it out? It won't come."

Newton didn't get a chance to respond before there was a banging on the door of the bus garage.

"Can you let them in?" asked Newton. "Check they're here for Smudge and then get them inside without letting any of the cats out."

Zaf opened the little door set into the large shutters. "Hello, can I help you?"

A woman stepped through. "I'm here because you might have my cat, Smudge."

"Great. Please, come this way. You need to go in this office, but without letting any cats out."

The woman was distracted by the number of cats in the large space of the bus garage. The bolder ones came to investigate her, wrapping themselves around her legs as they walked.

"What is this place?" she asked. "Why d'you have so many cats?"

"It's a funny story," said Zaf. "But let's see if we've got your cat first. In here."

Zaf took her into the office, where Newton was surrounded by nine black and white cats. Two of them hissed at each other on the floor, their backs arched and their tails erect as they faced off, stepping in slow motion. Another had tried to climb the wall. It swung on a framed certificate, its claws gripping the corner. The rest prowled around, looking agitated.

The woman stared around, her face a rictus of horror. "I can't believe what I'm seeing."

"It's not what it looks like," said Newton.

Zaf wasn't sure what it *did* look like.

"You're kidnapping pets to extort money from owners," the woman said. "I've heard about this. You steal them out of gardens."

"No! No, that's not what happened at all," Zaf said. "Tell her, Newton. It all just started with a tuna sandwich."

Newton sketched a curve with his hands to show the path of events. "There was a tuna sandwich, then some nice fresh sardines and somehow this is the result. I didn't set out to make these cats appear, they just liked the smell or something. Is your cat here, by the way?"

The woman stepped to the side to avoid the hissing pair of cats. They seemed to be escalating their skirmish. They moved in tighter circles, batting each other with extended paws. "Smudge isn't one of these cats."

"There's another one by the fridge," said Zaf. "I couldn't get it to come out. Come and have a look."

"I should report you, that's what I should do." The woman followed him anyway and peered into the gap as Zaf showed her where the cat was.

"Hello, Smudge!" She extended a hand and the cat walked out, purring.

Zaf grinned. "It's your kitty? That's wonderful news."

Zaf called out. "Newton, we have a satisfied customer!"

"I'm not satisfied with this situation," the woman said as she carried her cat away. "You can't treat people this way."

"What way?" asked Zaf, but she was already at the door.

Newton appeared at his side. "That's good then. One down."

Zaf looked around at the vast number of remaining cats. Some were sitting and cleaning themselves, some were growling at each other, and at least one was hacking up a furball.

He smiled at his colleague. "Yep. Definitely off to a good start."

But Newton seemed less happy. He was gazing towards the door.

"Why'd that woman assume that I was kidnapping cats and holding them for ransom?" he said.

"Some people can't accept a good deed for what it is."

"What?"

Zaf shrugged. "Everyone assumes there's an angle of some sort. People can't even do good deeds without thinking there's some catch."

"That seems very cynical," said Newton.

Zaf couldn't help but laugh. "People are cynical. I think you have a pleasantly simple view of things, Newton. I know you've got a life outside of this place but you also have a small and simple world in here, a world of buses." He hoped he hadn't been offensive.

Newton drew back. "Buses are complex creatures. You try dealing with the automatic remote mounted gearbox on a sixty-seven Routemaster!"

"I mean..." Zaf took a breath. "It's like homeless people. Trust me, I'm getting a bit of an insight at the moment. If you see a homeless person—"

"I offer to pop to the shops and get them something."

"Right. Some people are happy giving cash to the homeless, charities tell people it's better to give to projects that help them and there's a whole load of people out there who think that every homeless person is a con artist raking in money from the gullible and kind-hearted."

Newton tilted his head, acknowledging Zaf's point but not necessarily agreeing.

"And now," Zaf continued, "Diana's got this folder that seems to show this MP Chapman-Moore taking advantage of a new scheme to help the homeless. Line his own pockets.."

"That doesn't mean…" Newton indicated the door and the unhappy woman who'd just departed through it. "Just because there's some cynical and calculating people in the world, doesn't mean people can't be good for the sake of goodness."

Zaf patted his colleague on the shoulder. "And you *are* doing a good thing here."

Newton sniffed. "Be nice if people saw it for what it was."

# Chapter Forty-Five

Diana made her way to Parliament Square. As much as she loved walking, she didn't have the luxury of time this morning, so she caught the Jubilee Line from Baker Street to Westminster. Managing a not-quite-dry placard on the crowded tube was tricky.

"Are you doing a protest?" asked a woman with a backpack, revealing herself as a tourist by breaking the unspoken rule regarding talking to strangers on the underground.

"Not me personally," said Diana, feeling like that was a coward's answer. "Do you think I should?"

She crossed from the tube station and over to Parliament Square, and was pleased to find the small encampment of protesters still in place.

She recognised the woman, Giselle, she'd spoken to earlier in the week.

"Hi, remember me? Diana Bakewell, tour guide." She angled Zaf's placard, in case they hadn't noticed the massive cardboard sign. "My friend, Zaf, said he'd have a go at making a placard for you."

"This is amazing," Giselle said.

A small group gathered round to look at Zaf's work.

"Incredible picture!"

"Thank you so much for this."

"This looks just like my cat!"

Diana's head snapped round. "What? No! Really?"

The young man nodded. "Well, it was my parents' cat, until it ran away a few months ago."

"This is amazing news," said Diana. "Was your parents' cat, how can I put this? Was she—"

"A monster? Oh yes. Delilah – that's the cat – she'd wait up the garden for my mum to hang out the washing and then she'd leap out of the bushes just to claw her legs."

"That sounds like her."

And the dead things she'd bring in." He grimaced. "Rats, pigeons. You name it. And that's the sad thing really."

"The needless death," nodded Giselle.

"No. Well, yes, but the thing was, the cat brought them all as gifts. Excellent ratter, she was. She thought she was being a helpful house pet. I honestly believe she was showing my parents care and affection. In the most horrible way possible."

"Well, the good news is that I can tell your parents where she is," Diana said.

"Oh no, they don't want her back." The young man looked horrified. "They were relieved when she ran away, to be honest."

"Oh. Oh, OK."

It occurred to Diana that there were times when people didn't want to be reunited with former members of their families.

Families were odd things. Although she lived alone, Diana had a large extended family that spread across much of London like a web, with off-shoots further afield. There were aunts and uncles on almost every street corner of the East End. She had family members who lived almost their entire lives on the Thames, descendants of the ancient Watermen and Lightermen's Guild, now chugging back and forth in their stout tugboats. Diana had nothing but love for all of them.

Of course, there were people in her life who she'd fallen out and drifted away from – her old 'friend' Ariadne Webb, for example – but generally speaking, Diana's life was one of people who wanted to be together, who actually liked one another.

And then she thought of Ava Franks and the fact that John Chapman-Moore might well be her father. Even if that was true, that didn't mean Ava would want him in her life. Diana doubted the MP would either acknowledge Ava as his or even be a good father if he did.

"This is good," said Giselle, hoisting the placard higher. "Eye-catching. A few more coppers in the tin."

Diana looked around. "Your colleague, Catalina Arenosa, is she here?"

"Still being held for further questioning by the rozzers," said Giselle.

"Really?" From what Diana understood, the police could only hold someone without charge for twenty-four hours, in most cases.

"After the paint protest, they've got her on criminal damage and public nuisance charges. Potentially looking at a couple of years in prison."

"No. Really?"

Giselle tilted her head. "Maybe. Possibly suspended."

"That's a steep price to pay to protest."

"It's all about raising awareness. There're little things we can do but it's up to the lawmakers and the voting public to actually change things. Problem is, it's hard to get people to see that things can change."

"I can imagine," said Diana.

"Maybe there was a time when people respected our politicians, but confidence now is low."

Diana thought about John Chapman-Moore's crooked deal with homes for the homeless. The idealism expressed by some of the students stood in stark contrast to that.

"But there are people willing to fight the good fight," she said.

"Yes," replied Giselle. "But getting people to tell the difference between the honest and the evil is difficult."

There was a clink as someone threw money in the collection bucket.

"I bet you see the same people come by a lot," Diana said. "People who are keen to support. Who want to chat and but maybe not get involved."

"Maybe."

Diana took out her phone. She found the image she needed and zoomed in.

"What about this person? Sorry if it's a bit blurry."

"Oh, yeah, a frequent visitor," Giselle said. "Well, that's the point, isn't it? We want to catch people as they go in and out of Parliament."

She nodded at the grand edifice of the Palace of Westminster across the road.

"Thanks," said Diana. "That's very helpful."

She started to turn away then reconsidered and turned back to Giselle.

"I'd like to give you something, if you don't mind," she said and opened her bag to find her wallet.

## Chapter Forty-Six

Zaf wasn't keeping up with Newton's wall-based cat recording system at all. The string changed colour at certain points, but the reason why was known only to Newton. Nonetheless, the number of cats in the depot had fallen dramatically throughout the morning as people had come in to collect them.

"Can you get the door?" Newton asked him at lunchtime. "Mr and Mrs green-eyed-tortoiseshell are here. We might also have Mr Tinky Winky."

"Mr Tinky Winky?"

Newton shrugged. "I don't make the names up. We don't even know what kind of cat he's lost."

Zaf found the couple, as well as the man in the business suit who really didn't look like the kind of bloke who'd name his cat after a Teletubby. He ushered them all over to Newton.

"Welcome. You've lost a pair of tortoiseshells?" Newton asked the couple.

"Yes. They hardly ever go out beyond the garden. They're only young."

Newton went into the kitchen and returned with a pair of small cats that mewed piteously, as if rough streetwise cats had been making fun of them. "Is this them?"

"Oh yes!" exclaimed the woman. She took one from Newton and her husband took the other. "Thank goodness. We can get our babies home safe now."

The man in the suit came over and stared hard at the cat being held by the woman. "That there is my Tinky Winky! I'd know him anywhere."

"I can assure you this cat is mine," said the woman.

"It's definitely my Tinky Winky. Look how he responds when he hears my voice."

"It's because you're bellowing in his ears. It's not a positive response, it's cat PTSD." The woman angled her body to shield the cat.

Zaf and Newton exchanged a glance.

"This is definitely a case for the lap test," Newton said. "I'll take the cats and then you can all make your laps available, so we can see where the cats go."

"This is absurd," the woman said.

Newton convinced them all to sit on chairs in the kitchen while he and Zaf took the two cats. Diana had just returned, and stood watching from the doorway, shaking her head.

"Right, now Zaf, follow my lead," said Newton. "We'll walk to the far wall and turn the cats around so they can't see anyone's faces. I need to set some ground rules for you all, so listen carefully or the test will be invalid. You are not allowed to make any noises at all. In fact, it would be best if you all closed your eyes so you can't make eye contact. Keep them closed."

Zaf followed Newton, turned around, and released his cat.

The two cats trotted near to the chairs, then one sat down

to wash itself. The one that had been claimed by both parties jumped up onto the woman's lap, while the other one went to the man in the business suit.

"See! I told you," said the man in the suit.

"Wait a minute, that's the wrong one," said Zaf. "I know which was which, and you said the other one was Tinky Winky."

The man in the suit pulled a face. He looked more closely at the cat on his lap. "Oh."

Diana stepped forward from the doorway.

"Can I ask you both a question?" she said. "Whereabouts do you live?"

"Clarkes Mews."

"Twenty-one Upper Wimpole Street."

"Those roads back onto each other," she pointed out. "Maybe the cats have been spending time with both of you."

They all looked at each other. "It's possible," said the man in the suit.

The couple shrugged and nodded.

"Then I suggest you go back to whatever arrangement you already had, only now you'll be better informed," Diana said. "The cats have brought you together as neighbours."

They nodded and smiled at each other.

The man in the suit approached Newton. "These cats obviously aren't mine, I just borrow them sometimes. But it's made me realise I'd like one for myself. If you end up with any unclaimed, give me a call, yeah?"

"Will do," said Newton with a smile.

The three people left with the cats and Newton took down the related pictures.

"This scam John Chapman Moore is pulling," Zaf said. "It's a bit like that cat situation."

"One cat that everyone thought was two cats?"

"Creating a space for homeless people to move into and pretending it holds a lot more people than it really does."

"That place we visited, it's worse than that," said Diana. "That was zero accommodation, claiming to house hundreds."

"A massive scam. You reckon Hanna O'Grady's in on it?"

"Hmmm." Diana seemed unsure.

"Bet she's skimming thousands off the top in backhanders," he said.

Diana tutted "For the Serjeant at Arms at the House of Commons to be taking petty bribes... That'd be a low day for British democracy." She checked her phone. "Let's see what Paul Kensington's up to." She smiled. "He's driven up to Leicester. I've got a text saying he'll be out all day."

"That's good news. But we're done," Newton said.

Zaf spun around, searching. The depot was empty. "Have all of the cats gone? Really gone?"

Newton nodded. "All except Gus and Boudicca."

"Or Delilah, as her previous owners called her."

Newton and Zaf turned to stare at Diana.

"I found her owners," she explained. "Their son, anyway. They don't want her back."

"Wow, that is cold," said Newton, "but I suppose we need to let her out."

"Let her out of where?" Diana asked.

"She'd been getting a bit bitey with people coming in and taking the other cats away. It's like she's annoyed at losing her buddies."

"Buddies? She hates everyone," Zaf said. "Cats, humans, everyone."

"She isn't straightforward in showing affection," said Newton.

Diana nodded. "I'm starting to think that people, like cats, have an odd way of showing affection at times."

"Anyway," said Newton, "I shut her in the stationery cupboard while the last few people came. I should go and let her out."

They arrived at the stationery cupboard and Newton unlocked the door.

"Oh dear."

It was lucky the company didn't use much paper stationery these days. The contents of the cupboard had been ferociously shredded.

"Why did we even have this still?" Zaf lifted out a box of sprocket-holed printer paper. The top third had been converted into confetti.

"Not sure," said Newton. "But I have a more pressing question. There's one odd thing about this cupboard."

Zaf peered inside it.

"It doesn't have a cat in it," Newton continued.

"Oh, yeah. How did that happen? Has someone else let her out?"

Newton leaned right down to examine the bottom shelf. "I think she let herself out."

Zaf crouched down to look. There was a ragged hole at the back, showing brickwork and darkness beyond.

"That hole wasn't there before," he said. "Where does it even go? We know Boudicca likes exploring tunnels. She claimed your cat tower for herself after all."

"Not sure where it goes." Newton looked puzzled. "It seems to be angling down."

"But we've no idea where it leads," Diana said.

"Give me a minute," said Newton.

He went to a shelf and pulled down a folder. It was very

much a Newton folder, containing everything from wiring diagrams for the Routemaster to menus for the local takeaways. He flicked through until he found what he wanted. "Look at this."

Diana looked at a page which showed the route of part of the London Underground, with a street view superimposed on top.

"See how close the tunnel between Bond Street and Baker Street is to here?" Newton pointed out.

"I see," said Diana. She doubted Boudicca had made her way into the tunnels of the underground, but didn't say so.

"So we're just left with Gus now," Zaf said.

"He seems like a pleasant chap," Newton added.

Diana couldn't see the cat until Newton pointed him out. The big-boned grey cat with tufts of white fringing his face sat in the doorway of a bus.

"He looks at home," Zaf said.

"Speaking of homes and houses and such things, I have news," said Diana.

"Oh?"

"I know who killed Florence Breecher. And why."

# Chapter Forty-Seven

Zaf stared at Diana, jaw open.
"You do?"
She nodded.
"Tell us, then."

"Well," she said, "I suppose I'd best phone DCI Sugarbrook and tell him first. In the meantime, we've got a party of students to take to Parliament. The detective chief inspector can meet us there." She began to walk away. "Oh, and I ought to let Tabitha know."

Zaf looked at Newton, jaw still agape. "Does she often say she's solved murders?"

"Not to my knowledge," Newton replied, "but I don't like to pry into people's private lives." He moved towards the bus. "Right. Come on, Gus. Time to hop off. Newton's got to take the bus out."

In the short time it took the bus to make it out of the depot doors and travel the short distance up the road to the Redhouse Hotel, Gus had refused to get off it and Diana had refused to be drawn further on the matter of who had killed Florence

Breecher. Zaf found one of these things intensely entertaining and the other intensely annoying.

He greeted the Foxwood Grange students as they emerged from the hotel.

"Had a chilled morning? Ready for some parliamentary fun?"

"Is it ever fun?" said Ethan, climbing on board the bus.

"Might be today," Zaf muttered. He spotted Ava and gave her a supportive smile. "You OK with seeing him today?"

"Him?" she said, her brow furrowed. "Oh. Him." Her expression hardened. "I've seen him in the flesh now. I don't need him in my life."

"No."

The teachers were last. To Zaf's surprise, they did a headcount.

"All here," Zaf said. "Off we go!"

Newton drove while Diana took the microphone and gave a short overview of some of the sights en route. Her tone was distracted, and she was skipping some of the details. Zaf could tell her mind was elsewhere.

"Come on," he whispered to her. "You know who murdered Florence? Give us a clue."

"Clue? Honestly, the thing that clinched it for me was Boudicca."

"Boudicca?"

"Boudicca or Delilah. The demon cat."

"That's linked?"

"And then that got me thinking properly about Hanna O'Grady's walking stick."

"What about it?"

"She doesn't really need it. It's quite possible she doesn't need it at all."

Zaf tried to work out the relevance. "She got to the scene of the murder bloody quick, didn't she?"

"Exactly," Diana said. "But this whole thing is about homes and the ridiculous cost of living in London. I think *you* know something about that."

She looked into his eyes. Did she know where he'd slept last night?

The shed had been dusty and not exactly airy, but at least it had been cosy. It might well have been the best night's sleep he'd had for a while.

"Come on," she said, "we're here."

Newton pulled up to the drop-off point and the tour party piled off the bus onto the busy pavement. Diana led them round to the Cromwell Green entrance.

"Morning, Gillian," she said to the tall security woman.

"You really do know everyone in London, don't you?" Zaf said.

Diana said nothing, but smiled. They moved quickly through Westminster Hall and St Stephen's Hall and into Central Lobby where, unlike on their first visit, John Chapman-Moore MP was ready and waiting for them.

Azar Mirza was waiting beside him. Zaf wasn't sure why they were getting two Members of Parliament for the price of one, although if he had to spend time with one of them, he'd go for Azar every time.

"Ah, my young constituents." Chapman-Moore raised his deep voice and his meaty hands in greeting. "How nice to see you after all the brouhaha earlier in the week."

*Brouhaha*, thought Zaf. Did anyone really say that? Surely not to refer to the fatal stabbing of an employee and possible lover.

"Thank you for taking the time to speak to us," Diana said.

"It's a sombre occasion, returning here, but I hope we can find some solace and—"

"Yes," Chapman-Moore interrupted. "Our tour was curtailed last time. Let's see if we can pick up where we left off."

As he waved his hands to draw the students nearer, there was a shout of "Miss Bakewell!"

Zaf looked round to see the hulking figure of Detective Chief Inspector Sugarbrook striding down from the Common's Members' Lobby. Hanna O'Grady was beside him, her walking stick and shoes performing a complicated rhythm as she tried to keep up.

"What is this?" said Chapman-Moore. "I was about to do my famous tour of the Houses."

"And I need to talk to Miss Bakewell about murder," said Sugarbrook.

"Not without me," said Hanna O'Grady.

"Murder?" said Chapman-Moore.

Had he forgotten about Florence's murder?

"What's going on?" asked Ethan.

"Diana thinks she knows who killed the researcher," Ava told him.

Zaf stared at her.

"You two talk too loud on the bus," the girl said, "especially when you think no one's listening."

"You know who did it?" said another of the girls, Caitlin.

"This will just be a waste of time," Hanna O'Grady said. "I have important things to do and we don't need this kind of distraction."

"Yes," said Diana. "Getting distracted from work. That's what it's all about, oddly enough."

"If you have something to report," said Sugarbrook, a tone

of forced calm in his voice, "we should find a quiet place to discuss."

"You have to tell us, Miss," said Ethan.

Diana looked around the busy space. Her gaze snagged on something, but Zaf couldn't see what.

"Yes, let's find a better place to talk," she said. "Maybe this way."

She gave a little wave to bring the students with her, then set off along the tiled corridor.

"Where are we going?" Sugarbrook called.

"The Robing Room," Diana called back. "Where you corralled us all on Monday." She looked across at Zaf. "Zaf, did you ever find Merlin among all those engravings of Arthur and the Knights of the Round Table?"

"Er, no. We didn't."

"Funny that," she replied, with a knowing wink.

# Chapter Forty-Eight

The Robing Room was quiet. Diana could hear her heartbeat thrumming through her ears as they entered, her mind racing.

A group of foreign tourists were leaving as she turned to face her party of students, teachers, police officers and assorted people who worked in the Palace of Westminster.

"I'm not sure I intended to do it like this," she said, not sure now how she *had* imagined sharing her thoughts on Florence's death.

"This is not the way to assist a police investigation," grunted Sugarbrook.

"I want to hear what she has to say," said a student.

There was an impromptu but passionate chorus of *Yeahs*.

"Do you actually know who killed Florence?" asked Azar Mirza.

"I do."

Ethan eyed the students near him. "Are they in this room?"

"They are," Diana said.

This drew gasps.

Diana flinched. She hadn't wanted to make this sensational.

Sugarbrook went to the nearest door, moved the sash barriers and closed the door. Taking this as a cue, a security officer closed the doors at the other end of the room.

They were sealed in.

Sugarbrook turned and gave Diana a silent stare. She knew what was going through his mind: *Say your piece. Make a fool of yourself so I can get on with my job.*

Diana gave him a slow nod. She wasn't about to let him intimidate her.

"Very well." She cleared her throat, raising her voice so as to be heard by the whole group. "I should start off by saying I never knew Florence Breecher, never knew her as well as I might have liked. But I could tell she worked very, very hard. She was enthusiastic and diligent and filled with boundless energy. I think more than one person described her as a force of nature."

There were nods from Azar and Chapman-Moore.

"She was wild and impulsive. Her decisions were perhaps not the most sensible." Her gaze landed on the MP for Pudsey and Otley. "Were you having an affair with her, Mr Chapman-Moore?"

The MP spluttered and gasped. "Really?!"

"I don't know," she said. "You, Sir, have a reputation for using your position of power against young women. That reputation goes back to..."

She looked at Ava. The girl gave a small shake of her head.

Diana looked back at Chapman-Moore. "It goes back a long way."

"This is slander!" he said.

Azar sighed. "Oh, please."

Chapman-Moore looked to Hanna O'Grady for support. The Serjeant at Arms just looked at him, her expression giving nothing away.

"Dude, that's just pervy," said one of the boys.

"But Florence's choices were her own," said Diana. "She burned the candle at both ends and partied hard and didn't care who knew it. But she also had a fiercely strong moral streak. She wanted to do good. She wanted to help. I met a cat earlier—"

"A cat?" Ethan said.

"A cat. Called Boudicca or Delilah. Poor thing drove its owners mad with its violence and its habit of bringing dead rats to their door. I'm sure Boudicca thought she was doing good, being helpful, but it was enough to drive the owners mad."

"Weren't you gonna tell us who killed the woman?" Ethan said.

"Right, right." Diana cleared her throat. "Someone murdered Florence Breecher. Someone went into Mr Chapman-Moore's office, took his brass letter opener from his desk, and then, at some point later, stabbed Florence in the back while everyone was distracted by the protestor, Catalina Arenosa. What annoyed me at first was that the police seemed to be more worried about Mr Chapman-Moore and the other politicians."

"Every individual is of equal importance to the police," Sugarbrook said.

"It doesn't always feel that way. Everyone focuses on the big, noisy, *important* people. The little people in the background are easily overlooked. You said yourself, Zaf, how easy it is to feel invisible in a huge city like this."

Zaf nodded.

"But even people in the spotlight can work invisibly if

they're careful," Diana continued. "John Chapman-Moore has been running a property scam in London for some time. The pilot programme for his Helping Hands for the Homeless bill has allowed him to claim thousands of pounds for housing hundreds of non-existent homeless people in properties that aren't even habitable."

"Double slander!" Chapman-Moore roared.

Hanna O'Grady gave him a steely glare.

"Florence knew," Diana said. "She compiled a folder of evidence. John, I don't know if you were even aware that your closest employee was building up a stash of evidence against you."

"This is all lies!"

"It's true," said Diana. "The Serjeant at Arms knew about it, too."

Diana glanced at Hanna O'Grady, expecting a reaction. Hanna's expression remained calm.

"Hanna," Diana said, "you told me you'd never met Florence Breecher. But a note in her diary indicated she visited you at your private members' club on Sunday, the day before she died." She licked her lips. "I went in and checked. She'd signed in to see you."

## Chapter Forty-Nine

Zaf looked from Diana to Hanna O'Grady and back again.

There was still no change in Hanna's expression. The group was quiet, waiting for the Serjeant at Arms's reply.

"She came to you with a folder of evidence," Diana said. "On the Monday, I saw you and Mr Chapman-Moore talking. I think you were discussing his fraudulent activity."

"Dodgy git!" muttered one of the students.

"Were you going to blackmail him?" Diana asked, looking at Hanna. "Is that why you rejected the folder Florence brought to you? Was Florence getting in the way of you skimming some money off John Chapman-Moore's crooked deal?"

Hanna barked out a laugh. "This is amateur hour, is it? If you must know, I presented the evidence to the Metropolitan Police two days ago—"

"What?" Chapman-Moore's eyes bulged.

Hanna's gaze on Diana was steely. "You approached me at choir practice, Miss Bakewell. Trying to question me. Pretty ham-fisted, I'd say."

Zaf's throat was dry. He hadn't expected Diana to reveal everything like this. But the students were rapt: best part of the trip, as far as they were concerned.

Maybe the police detective would chip in now to confirm or deny it.

Instead Diana carried on talking.

"Oh, well that explains everything," she said.

"Does it?" Hanna said.

"Does it?" DCI Sugarbrook said.

"It does," Diana replied. "You see, there was something my colleague Zaf pointed out to me."

All eyes shifted to Zaf. He shrank back, trying to remember.

"The folder I was given," said Diana. "Florence's folder. There was a glossy brochure for Mr Chapman-Moore's property. The important details were highlighted. And the reports from Companies House had Mr Chapman-Moore's name highlighted, too. In pretty little asterisks, quite distinctive."

Zaf had a vague memory of her pointing something similar out when they'd left that caff last night.

She gave a small smile. "Why would Florence do that? If the folder was just for her, she wouldn't have needed to highlight anything. But it was obvious enough. The same applies if she intended to give it to the Serjeant at Arms or the police."

"I told you she already gave me the folder," Hanna said.

"Yes. And you took it. So this *different* folder was intended for a *different* audience, for a *different* purpose."

"Well, let's see it then," snapped Chapman-Moore. "I'll not let my good name be abused if my accusers can't present evidence."

"I don't have it anymore," Diana's tone was breezy. The students were muttering around Zaf. "I gave it away, to some people who I'm sure will make good use of it. Mr Chapman-Moore, I suspect your time as an MP might be drawing to an end."

"Threats now, eh?"

"I don't think your electorate will want you representing them." Diana spread her arms to indicate the students.

"School children?" he scoffed.

"Many of them old enough to vote, soon. Old enough to stand for your seat." Diana cast a glance at Ava.

"But Miss Bakewell," said Sugarbrook, "you're saying the folder Florence gave you isn't her original folder of evidence."

"It's not," she said. "Which is odd. There'd be no need for two, would there? And then I thought of Ms O'Grady's walking stick." She pointed at the Serjeant at Arms's cane with her brolly.

"What about it?" Hanna snapped.

"You don't need it."

"I told you as much. It's not a secret."

"But you still carry it. Why?"

"In case I *do* need it. I broke my leg years ago, and I still get twinges."

"*And* you told me it was good, other people seeing you had a cane. It meant that they got out of your way, made allowances for you. Yes?"

Zaf waited. Was she going to tell them how this all linked together?

"It's like when people phone in sick to work," Diana said. "Even when we're really ill, we still put on the *poorly* voice. Hanna O'Grady suffers with mobility problems but carries an unnecessary walking stick to make sure everyone knows."

"And?" said Hanna.

"The folder I was given was a fake, a new fabrication. Like

Ms O'Grady's stick, it's a signal. It was designed *only* to draw fresh eyes to John Chapman-Moore's corruption."

"Am I going to stand here and be insulted all day?" cried Chapman-Moore.

"Obviously, yes," said Azar. "Just shut up. You're an embarrassment to yourself."

"The folder I was given was a fake, and the real one already existed," said Diana. "It was created so that anyone looking at it might think Mr Chapman-Moore had murdered his researcher to silence her."

She gestured around her. "Almost everyone here was present when Florence was stabbed. Almost everyone here had access to the office and the letter-opener." She paused. "But the murder was only successful because it coincided with a noisy, attention-grabbing protest by Ms Arenosa."

Diana cocked her head. Zaf was impressed by the way she was holding the crowd. "It's quite a coincidence," she said. "Unless it was planned that way."

"The protestors did it," said Ethan.

"No," Diana said. "Catalina Arenosa was so committed to non-violence that she bought vegan paint for her attack."

"So, not a coincidence, and not pre-planned..." said Zaf.

"Oh, it was premeditated alright," said Diana. "But Catalina Arenosa didn't know the whole plan. Her accomplice helped her source the paint, helped her decide on the timing of her attack, perhaps even gave advice on sneaking the paint into the Palace of Westminster."

"You know all this?" Sugarbrook asked.

Diana nodded. "Zaf showed me a selfie the other day. I spotted someone in the background. I phoned the paint suppliers this morning because I saw the vegan *Bambubu* pens in their window. You can get vegan pens, too. Who knew?

Quite a coincidence, given that shop is the only stockist for those pens in the entire country. And then later this morning, I spoke to the protestors in Parliament Square. I showed them Zaf's picture and the person in the background. They confirmed that she'd spoken to Catalina many times."

She looked across the people around them.

*Who?* Zaf thought back to taking that photo. *Who had been there?*

Diana looked over the group. "Tabitha Welkin," she said.

There were frowns. The students looked around at each other.

They were all thinking the same: *Who?*

But Zaf knew the name: Tabitha was Florence's cousin and housemate. Or had been.

The one studying for exams.

But she wasn't with them.

He watched Diana's gaze travel to the back of the group. He straightened up to see where she was looking.

He was wrong.

There she was. Tabitha Welkin, standing at the back of the group, dressed in the green tunic of the palace cleaning staff.

"Tabitha," Diana said, "you murdered your cousin, and you did it in a room full of witnesses. And," she sighed, "the astonishing thing is that you almost got away with it."

# Chapter Fifty

Tabitha stared at Diana. No one moved.

Diana broke the silence.

"Tabitha, you told me you found that folder of evidence among Florence's things. That's not true. You made it yourself. I recognised the little flower asterisks. They're just like the ones on a small ad we saw in a café in Bethnal Green last night. Little flowers you drew with that *Bambubu* pen you had on you when we met. The pen you bought at the same shop where you told Catalina to get her vegan paint."

"It's not like that," said Tabitha. Her voice was strained and she looked like she might cry. "I put the folder together, yes. But only because it was important that someone knew."

"Important that suspicion was directed at someone other than you," said Diana. "What was it you said when you gave me that folder? *I don't want to be seen to be interfering.* You didn't want to be seen – yet that need to drive attention elsewhere was the one thing that drew my attention to you. You should have relied on the one quality you seem to have in abundance."

"Quality?" Zaf said.

Diana turned to him. "Invisibility. A cleaner is almost entirely invisible. Tabitha told us she worked here on the facilities team. You, Zaf, said that a cleaner or a security guard or any worker could have got into Mr Chapman-Moore's office. We passed Tabitha several times that first day, but did we notice? She's in that photograph, cleaning the brass doorhandles in St Stephen's Hall. That smell clinging to the folder she gave us, the smell that seemed to follow us everywhere: brass polish."

"I don't know her," said Chapman-Moore. "She's nothing to do with me. I didn't put her up to it or anything!"

"That's the problem with people like you," Tabitha spat. "You think everything's about you."

"Florence's death had nothing to do with her work, did it?" Diana said. "Not directly. And it had absolutely nothing to do with you, Mr Chapman-Moore."

"Then what?" DCI Sugarbrook said.

"Holding down a job and completing a university course is hard, isn't it?" Diana said, addressing Tabitha. "I wouldn't know – never done it myself – but I bet it is. The thought of having to retake a year..."

"She flunked her exams," Zaf said.

"But she didn't flunk them." Diana turned to Tabitha. "Did you? You worked really hard. But how hard was it to work or even sleep with a housemate like Florence? The party animal. Coming and going at all hours. Disturbing the light-sleeping Tabitha."

"Really?" Azar said. "That's not a motive to kill someone. You could just—"

"Move out?" suggested Diana. "Not all of us have that luxury. The saddest thing, or one of the saddest things, is that

Florence thought she was being a good housemate. The parties. Putting on a bit of a *do* for poor Tabitha. Like a cat bringing an endless supply of dead rat presents to its increasingly horrified owners."

"So this woman killed her?" said Hanna O'Grady.

"This woman – Tabitha – was desperate. She made a plan. She knew there was a knife in John Chapman-Moore's office. She cleaned the place often enough. She struck up a conversation with the protestors. She egged Catalina on and helped her find the paint from a shop Tabitha already knew. She took the time to create a folder of evidence pointing the finger at someone else, evidence she knew about because Florence had been complaining about her boss for weeks." Diana licked her lips. "And on Monday, while we were all distracted by Catalina's protest, Tabitha stepped out of the background and stabbed her cousin in the back."

"I loved her!" Tears streamed down Tabitha's face. "I couldn't... I didn't..."

"I know," Diana said. "I saw you that evening. You were genuinely upset. You sought me out. Maybe that was just guilt. I don't know."

She turned to look along the panel of wood carvings on the Robing Room wall. She saw the one she wanted and stepped towards it.

"King Arthur and Mordred. We spent a lot of time cooped up in this room after the attack. And – was it you, Ethan? – you asked me why Arthur was reaching out his hand for Mordred, even though they'd just mortally wounded one another in battle." She looked at Tabitha. "Because even after they destroyed each other, there was still love there."

Diana sniffed and took a breath. She was done.

DCI Sugarbrook approached Tabitha. "Miss, perhaps we need to have a bit of a chat..."

Tabitha blinked her tears away, her eyes widening.

Chapman-Moore opened his mouth to complain about the whole business. The Serjeant at Arms drew him to a corner of the room, a look of fury on her face.

Azar approached Diana. "Do all your tours end this way?"

"That's what I was gonna ask," said Zaf.

Diana looked between them. She shook her head. "I think this one should end with tea and cake in the Westminster café and you, Azar, giving the students some tips on what they should do if they'd like to run for parliament."

She led the way to the door, umbrella in hand. The parliament security guard opened it for them as they went through.

"Thank you, Gillian," Diana said.

# Chapter Fifty-One

Friday morning was quiet in the Chartwell and Crouch bus depot. Down the road, the students and teachers of Foxwood Grange Academy would be getting ready for their return journey to Otley.

Paul Kensington was back in the depot office. He had told them, at some length and volume, how he had been 'parachuted in to troubleshoot some issues with a Leicester company'. Diana secretly wished she could have been a fly on the wall for that.

But the important thing was that the depot was back in order. Paul's little Zen garden had been topped up with fresh sand and raked into a pattern that didn't include scuffed paw prints.

The place felt odd, now it wasn't filled with every housecat from within a half-mile radius. Empty.

Newton was working on repairs to a wobbly headlight on the vintage Routemaster bus. The big grey tom cat, Gus, sat in the doorway, alternating between washing himself and watching Newton.

"He loves the bus," Newton told Diana. "Loves riding around on it. I think it's the motion or something."

"Aren't you afraid he'll get off and run away?" she asked.

"I don't think so. I think he's decided he lives here now."

"Has Paul noticed him yet?"

Newton looked around, then shook his head. "I swear Paul has looked straight at Gus a few times, but he acted like nothing was different."

"Good," said Diana. "Then I guess he lives here now."

She went into the kitchen to make herself a cup of tea. There were the schedules for next month's tours to organise. One of the big West End theatres intended to lay on an authentic 'London Experience' for some visiting foreign investors, and Diana wanted to get some ideas down before Paul even mentioned the awful-sounding Londiniumarium idea again.

As she entered the kitchen, Zaf was rinsing out the teapot.

"Morning," she said.

"Morning."

"Sleep well?"

He shrugged. "You lied to me."

"Oh?"

Zaf filled the teapot with water from the wall-mounted boiling water tank.

"You told me your area of expertise was London."

"It is."

He shook his head. "I think it's solving mysteries."

She waved his suggestion away. "There's no skill to it."

"Really?" He put cups on the table: a mug for him, a cup and saucer for Diana.

"You accused me of knowing everyone in London," she

said. "I really don't. People, mysteries. It's just about taking the time to notice things, keeping your eyes and ears open."

"Uh-huh."

She stroked the handle of her cup. "For example, I can't help noticing you're homeless, Zaf."

He put the teapot down heavily.

"And your failure to answer my question just now," she continued, "tells me you're not getting a decent night's sleep in that shed."

She watched his back. He was standing at the counter, hand on the teapot. Choosing between lies and excuses, maybe.

He turned to her. "The potting table's more comfortable than you'd think."

She didn't believe a word of it. "You need to stop sleeping in there. I've, er... I've got a big place for just one person." She held up a hand before he could speak. "I've got used to my own space. And I don't need a lodger. But... just for the short term."

"You're magic, Diana!" His face lit up.

She shrugged. "We may both come to regret this."

His grin didn't shift all the time he poured the tea.

"I've got to show you something." He sat down beside her, phone in hand. He angled the screen round and tapped play on a news video. The tickertape along the bottom read *Disgraced MP in property fraud revelations*. There were images of John Chapman-Moore, stock images of houses and rent signs, and then footage of Giselle and Catalina and the other anti-poverty protestors, talking to an unseen interviewer.

Zaf looked at Diana. "You gave the folder to the protestors."

"I hoped they'd go public."

"Even though the folder was a fake."

"A fake version of a real thing."

He looked down at the screen again. "Look at this."

Centre-screen, not exactly dominating things but very much present, was Zaf's fat cat placard.

"Fame, of sorts." Diana smiled.

He gave a noncommittal shrug. "Speaking of cats..." He swiped away and pulled up another video.

He pressed play. A man in a Transport for London tabard was talking to the camera.

"Well, we do have a rat problem here at Baker Street underground station. People drop far too much litter, and it encourages the little so-and-sos. But we've seen something new these past few days."

The video cut to wobbly camera footage, taken at the edge of the underground platform. Passengers waiting for an arriving train were startled by the arrival of a small pack of rats being chased down the platform by an enormous tan and black cat.

"Delilah?" asked Diana.

"Or Boudicca," Zaf replied.

There was another cut, to a man and a woman talking to the interviewer.

"Oh, look it's Edgar and Anastasia," Diana said.

Zaf gave her a disbelieving look.

"They were supposed to meet on a blind date at Victoria earlier this week."

He scoffed. "You don't have to make things up, just so you can seem knowledgeable."

The happy couple, hip to hip, shared the story of their encounter with Baker Street's new resident ratter. Their names appeared in a strip at the bottom.

"Anastasia and Edgar," said Zaf. "Diana, you *do* know everyone in London!"

"I'm magical, remember," she said and sipped her tea.

* * *

Thank you for reading *Death at Westminster*. You can read more about Diana and Zaf in *The Eccleston Square Mystery*, in which Diana must solve a mystery right at her own front door. Get your free copy at rachelmclean.com/eccleston.

# Read the London Cosy Mysteries Series

*Death at Westminster*

*Death in the West End*

*Death at Tower Bridge*

*Death on the Thames*

...and more to come

Buy from book retailers or via the Rachel McLean website.

# Also by Rachel McLean

**The DI Zoe Finch Series** – buy from book retailers or via the Rachel McLean website.

*Deadly Wishes*

*Deadly Choices*

*Deadly Desires*

*Deadly Terror*

*Deadly Reprisal*

*Deadly Fallout*

*Deadly Christmas*

*Deadly Origins*, the FREE Zoe Finch prequel

**The Dorset Crime Series** – buy from book retailers or via the Rachel McLean website.

*The Corfe Castle Murders*

*The Clifftop Murders*

*The Island Murders*

*The Monument Murders*

*The Millionaire Murders*

*The Fossil Beach Murders*

*The Fossil Beach Murders*

*The Blue Pool Murders*

*The Lighthouse Murders*

*The Ghost Village Murders*

**The McBride & Tanner Series** – Buy from book retailers or via the Rachel McLean website.

*Blood and Money*

*Death and Poetry*

*Power and Treachery*

...and more to come

**The Cumbria Crime Series by Rachel McLean and Joel Hames** – Buy from book retailers or via the Rachel McLean website.

*The Harbour*

*The Mine*

*The Cairn*

...and more to come

# Also by Millie Ravensworth

**The Cozy Craft Mysteries** – Buy now in ebook and paperback

*The Wonderland Murders*

*The Painted Lobster Murders*

*The Sequinned Cape Murders*

*The Swan Dress Murders*

*The Tie-Dyed Kaftan Murders*

*The Scarecrow Murders*

Printed in Great Britain
by Amazon